A STRANGER IN
FEATHERWOOD FALLS

HEATHER REYBURN

Cover design: Patti Roberts

ISBN 978-0-6451234-7-0 Print Edition

Heather Reyburn

www.heatherreyburn.com

For my husband, Roger

1

On a cool autumn evening exactly eleven months and twenty-nine days after the worst day of her life, Ginny Shepherd dropped the final spoonful of peanut brownie mix onto a tray. Crossing the old-fashioned kitchen, she slid the biscuits into the oven, folded her arms, and met the contemplative eyes of the black cat at her feet.

'What do you think I should have done, Oscar? I know he's not here, but they were his favourites and tomorrow I can sit on the step and gaze across the paddock while I dunk one in my tea—just like he and I did this time a year ago.'

'Meow.'

Ginny picked him up and rubbed her cheek against his soft fur. 'What would I do without you lot, eh?' A deep rumbling purr resonated from the cat's chest and she lowered him to the floor. 'Come on then. I'll feed you before I lock up the chooks.'

She scooped a cup of dry cat biscuits from the plastic container and dropped them into the bowl. Leaning against the veranda door, she waited as two more cats appeared, bending their heads together rattling the kibble around the dish. Leaving them contentedly eating, she stepped into a pair of gumboots and hurried into the fading light.

As she reached the wooden gate leading from the garden to the house paddock, her brow creased and she paused, lifting her gaze to the ridge behind the house. In the still air, the sound of cascading water drifted toward her. Peeping sounds and leaves rustling in the mock orange hedge signalled birds settling down for the night.

'What really happened? You had so much to live for,' she whispered. The lump that never seemed to leave completely, grew heavy inside her.

Her step slowed as she reached the fowl pen. Closing the gate, she slid the bolt as a chilly gust swept her shoulder length hair into her face. She rubbed her upper arms and shivered. Something didn't feel right. Was he trying to tell her something? A dog barked from the row of kennels twenty metres away and she strode toward the sound.

Opening the latch on the first pen, she swung the gate and rubbed the side of the kelpie's face. Yellow eyebrows shone against the dog's deep red coat and her tail rapped furiously against the mesh as she squirmed with excitement.

'Come, Flute. You can sleep on the veranda tonight and keep me company.' The dog leapt out of her cage and ran in circles around her mistress while hopeful yips and whines emanated from the other kennels. Ginny walked down the row, speaking to each as she went. 'You've had a good run today—and eaten your dinner. I'll be back in the morning.'

As she and Flute turned their backs and walked toward the house, silence once again reigned.

A shrill ring reverberated across the lawn and Ginny ran, leaping up the steps before wrenching the French door open.

'Hello?' She held one hand against her chest to still her pulse while she took slow breaths.

'Mum? Where have you been? This is the third time I've rung.'

'Briony. Sorry, darling. I nipped out to lock up the chooks and took longer than I planned.' A nutty, chocolate smell drifted around the open living area and Ginny glanced anxiously across the room. 'Hang on a sec. I'd better get the brownies out of the oven before they burn.' She dropped the receiver beside the vase of roses on the dining table and hurried to the stove. Seconds later, she picked up the handpiece and frowned.

'It's very early over there. Are you alright?'

'Yeah. I'm okay. I woke early and have been on the laptop for over an hour trying to get a flight home.' The girl's voice shook with emotion, and Ginny raised her eyebrows.

'Do you think you might be better staying put?' Ginny's reassurance wavered. 'You're a long way from populated areas. Maybe you could wait out the summer and try again after this confusion settles down?'

A flood of tears met her suggestion, and Ginny ached with sympathy for her daughter.

'I just want to come home, Mum,' Briony hiccupped. 'Especially now. It-it's a year tomorrow since ...'

Ginny slumped onto the couch, steeling herself before she spoke. 'I know. I miss him too and there's nothing I'd like more than to have you girls here with me. But that's not possible until this pandemic is under control—or at least until we all know more about how to deal with it.'

'Have the police contacted you again?'

'No. Last I heard it was still an open case though— so who knows?' Ginny switched the phone to her other ear as she rose and began transferring the cooling biscuits onto a wire rack. 'How's Alex?'

A huff of breath echoed through the receiver, and Ginny blinked.

'He's fine. Of course, he doesn't want me to leave. Says the Isle of Skye is the best place for both of us to sit it out—especially as the tourist season is just kicking off here.' Briony snorted. 'Fat lot of good that will be if Scotland locks everyone down like Australia did.'

Ginny twisted her mouth and squared her shoulders. 'Let's not go there. You've got a good job—at least for this season, anyway. And you've got Alex and a cosy cottage to live in.'

Briony groaned. 'You're right—as usual. I'm thinking of you though, Mum, and I wish I was home, sitting on the veranda and eating your delicious peanut brownies instead of planning the menus for the week.'

'I'll eat an extra one and think of you,' Ginny said with a soft smile.

'How's Grandma?'

Ginny grinned to herself. 'She's fine. A bit annoyed at not being able to get out and about—or have visitors. Thank goodness she bought that iPad. Apparently Ryan, the young fellow who's been teaching her how to use it sends her messages every day. He's taught her how to play games and she's forever on her Facebook page.'

Briony's spluttered laughter echoed in Ginny's ear.

'She'll be miles ahead of you then, Mum.'

'That's not hard. You forget how poor our internet

connection is here. Anyway, even if it was good, I doubt I'd have a fraction of the time to spend on it that she does.' Ginny huffed. 'Still, she's pretty good for eighty-two, isn't she?'

'Sure is. Give her my love when you ring. And tell her to invite me to be one of her Facebook friends.'

'I will.'

'Thanks Mum. I suppose I'd better go.'

'Thanks for ringing, love. Have a good day at the lodge. Perhaps today you'll meet some nice new guests to take your mind off things?'

'Yeah, sure. I'll ring you if I have any luck with flights.'

'Okay. Talk again soon. Bye.'

'Bye.'

Ginny replaced the receiver. There was nothing she would like more than to have her two girls home with her—especially now. She missed her husband so much. Lyndon had been a good father. He had been a wonderful husband—and the unfairness of his sudden death still tore at Ginny's heart.

She rose and returned to the bench. Lifting the lid off the cookie jar, she layered as many as would fit inside, then stored the rest in a battered biscuit tin with a picture of a Labrador on the lid. Then she microwaved remnants of cottage pie from the previous night, switched on the television, and curled up in the armchair.

Once we've got through tomorrow, I'll be better, she convinced herself. *It's always hard for the first year.* But something puzzled her and she couldn't put her finger on what it was. Lyndon was so careful. So methodical. His accident made no sense.

2

*D*awn broke the following morning as grey and dull as Ginny's sentiments.

'Buck up, girl.' She chided herself and slid out of the enormous bed, then crossed to the French doors opening onto the veranda. Flute lay on the mat outside, peering through the glass at Ginny and flapping her tail against the timber floor. Ginny pushed the door wide and bent to pat her. 'Thanks for keeping me company, girl. I knew you'd do a good job as a sentry. Let me get dressed and have coffee first. Then we'll let your mates out for a run.'

She peeled off her nightie and stepped into the shower. Half an hour later, her freshly washed brown hair clipped back at the nape and wearing clean jeans and shirt, her mood improved. Aided by a cup of coffee and the hint of sunshine peeping through the trees,

Ginny picked up the scrap bucket, slipped her arms into a quilted vest and headed outside. With Flute bounding alongside her, she fed the chooks before continuing to the kennels.

'How's my orchestra this morning?' A cacophony of excited barks responded, and she walked along the row of pens, throwing each gate open. As the team of kelpies dashed off to find a suitable patch of ground to use as a toilet, the hint of a smile touched her lips. No matter how tough the year had been, her animals had been a comfort. Even Drum, the youngest dog and Lyndon's favourite, had adjusted to her instruction— most of the time, anyway.

'Here Drum! Here Banjo! Here Harp!'

Three black and tan kelpies bounded back to her, dropping at her feet, and she turned to where Chime and Flute were sniffing around the base of the ancient Casuarina tree that shaded the kennels.

'Are you coming to the Falls with me?'

As though blue-toothed, five pairs of eyes glanced at her before facing the well-worn track.

'Off you go.' Drum trotted at her side while the other four dogs raced ahead, disappearing into the patch of bush.

Scrambling over the granite rise, Ginny followed them down the other side before climbing the final few metres to a lush pocket of ancient rainforest. One hundred and twenty years earlier, Lyndon's great-grandfather had received the deeds for Featherwood Station, accepting the deal permitted logging of native timber to continue for years—an agreement that subsequent generations regretted. The tiny clump around Ginny's favourite section of the water course was all that remained.

With the breeze in her face, fine spray reached Ginny seconds before tumbling water over a haphazard array of rocks appeared in view. She stood beside the larger of two pools and leaned against a solid granite boulder. Gazing down the slope, her stare followed the spread of vegetable fields and orchards before resting on the tiny township of Featherwood Falls.

Squinting, she studied the acres of celery lining the creek dividing Featherwood Station and her neighbouring property, Glenrowan. Bush partially hid the track through the bottom paddock of Featherwood Station, leading west along Glenrowan's boundary where, on the topmost ridge, scrub vied with granite outcrops. At the summit, in amongst the smooth, grey stone, the headwaters of a second stream seeped from a natural spring, traversed the steep slope, and joined the creek in a perfect Y shape, increasing in pace as it flowed into a sparkling lake at the edge of the property.

Ginny turned toward the shadowy fold of land behind her, where the bush skirted the track, hiding the cutting. Generations had witnessed the slow shift of two enormous boulders, allowing a pass to be created, wide enough to drive stock through and eliminating the additional two kilometre journey along the gentler country of the valley. Directly below the cutting, the land fell away to the creek, twenty metres below—where she had found Lyndon on that fateful day.

Shuddering, she returned her focus to the cluster of buildings in the valley and drew a sudden breath.

'Cripes. It's the first Monday of the month and I promised Lola I'd help with the tuck shop orders.'

She called the dogs and took a last glance at the cascading stream. Sparkling in the morning sunshine, the water appeared from amongst the bush and poured over rocks, bubbling and dark, the colour of weak black tea.

With water and timber abounding and wide swathes of clear land for crops or grazing, it made sense to Ginny that the area had been one of the first inland areas to be settled. She could not have imagined living anywhere more perfect—until now.

REFUSING to cast more than a fleeting glimpse at the tarpaulin-covered heap in the corner of the shed, Ginny lifted the empty fuel container into the boot, slid behind the steering wheel and reversed out.

Having quickly discovered how much petrol was required for the maintenance of Lyndon's precious expanse of lawn, she was looking forward to the frosty weather approaching. A period of slow grass growth where time spent roaring around on the ride-on mower would ease and remembering to fill the jerry can every couple of weeks could be shelved until spring.

She turned off the dirt track onto the main bitumen road that wound into the valley and parked beside the General Store. Scooping up the biscuit tin, she slung her bag over her shoulder and walked inside, stepping around Boris, the geriatric blue heeler that lay beside the door mat.

'Hello, my dear!' Lola's enthusiastic tone brought a smile to Ginny's face, and she leaned forward to be engulfed in the older woman's embrace. 'I know I shouldn't really be doing this, what with all this social distancing and stuff. But today, of all days, I think we can ignore the rules. We all need a hug at times like this,' Lola whispered. 'Are you okay?'

Ginny stepped back and nodded silently. Sympathy filled Lola's eyes and Ginny had to swallow to prevent tears from rolling down her cheeks. Her friend remembered despite her busy workload and it gave her heart a lift.

'Here, I made a batch of peanut brownies yesterday, so I brought some to have for our morning tea.'

'Oh, you are a dear.' Her round, cheerful face looked up at Ginny as she grasped the container. 'You know you don't need to do that.' Lola waved an arm in the air. 'We have a shop full of food.' Then she chuckled and brushed a loose, grey strand of hair off her face. 'Thank you. Frank will be chuffed. You know how he loves his tucker.'

Ginny smiled and drew a deep breath. 'Right. What needs to be done?'

Lola bustled toward the rear of the shop and lifted the folding section of countertop for Ginny to pass under. 'We'll get on with the sandwich orders first. I've made pasties because of the cooler weather, but one child wants a salad roll, so I'll leave that to you while I mash the eggs.'

Ginny nodded and followed Lola into the spacious kitchen behind the shop front. Removing an apron from a hook behind the door, the older woman passed it to Ginny before opening the fridge and handing her a tray of sliced ham and a tub of margarine.

While they talked, they ticked the sandwich orders off the list, wrapped and labelled the packets, then stacked them neatly in the fridge. The front doorbell tinkled and Lola snatched up a sanitising wipe and rubbed it over her hands. 'I'll deal with that while you make the salad roll.'

'Sure.' Ginny's interest piqued as she heard the delight in Lola's welcome. She took a sideways step so she could see the customer through the open door. A pretty young woman dressed in a smart navy blue suit stood in the middle of the shop, her bright lipstick matching the flash of red nails as she bent down to hug Lola. It was obvious the visitor was both familiar to Lola and someone she hadn't seen for a while.

Ginny dropped her gaze to the table and finished assembling the roll while she listened to their exuberant greeting.

'I'm on a round trip with work, visiting each of our branches to put a face to a name. You know how it is these days—everyone's getting jittery about the safety of their jobs and it's my role as human resources officer to reassure them ... at least for the moment, anyway.' Her voice trailed off as Lola grasped her arm and dragged her toward the kitchen.

'Perfect timing. I've got a friend giving me a hand with the weekly school tuck shop orders.' She laughed. 'Not that it's a big job—twenty-five kids doesn't take long to sort out. Mind you, add the principal and his wife, teacher aide and the admin assistant and it still takes a bit of planning.' She rambled on before stopping in front of Ginny. 'Ginny, meet my niece, Katrina.'

Ginny reached out her hand, quickly withdrawing it when Katrina held up her elbow. 'Oh sorry, we're still getting used to these new *acceptable methods of greeting*.' She responded with a brief touch of sleeved elbow. 'We're hardly aware of the pandemic out here, you see

—so we need reminding. Anyway, I'm Ginny.' She smiled at Katrina while Lola fussed around putting the kettle on and setting out mugs.

Within a few minutes, Ginny's biscuit tin lay open on the table and she sipped her tea while Lola bombarded Katrina with questions and information about people Ginny didn't know. Her mind drifted back to the last morning tea she had shared with her husband. Suddenly conscious of Katrina asking her something, she jerked back to the present and gathered her wits.

'I'm sorry, Katrina. I was miles away. What did you say?'

'I wondered if you have children at the school.' She pointed to the tuck shop order on the table beside her.

'Oh no. My girls are in their twenties now. One in Scotland and the other in Sydney. I guess I got in the habit of helping Lola years ago when they were home —and haven't stopped.'

'You must miss them. Especially now.' She looked sheepishly at Lola. 'Aunty Lol mentioned your husband has died. Do you get lonely?'

Ginny swallowed and wrapped both hands around her mug, contemplating Katrina's observations. Was she that transparent? Of course not. *I'm just ... lost.* She gave a small shake of her head. 'I'm not lonely, but life is certainly not the same. Sometimes I wonder if I'll ever get used to it.'

Lola covered Ginny's hand with her own work-worn palm and squeezed it gently.

'If you don't mind me asking, what did your husband die of?' Katrina asked.

Ginny stared at her in surprise. In towns this size, she knew secrets were impossible to keep and warmth filled her soul as she swung her glance to Lola. Her husband's death would have been the topic on many lips in the pub, General Store and Post Office—the latter two operated by Lola and her patient husband of almost fifty years. All venues were hotbeds of gossip. This time, she was grateful to her friend for keeping silent, at least to her family.

'My husband was killed in a quad bike accident on our farm.'

'I'm so sorry, Ginny.' Katrina tilted her head to one side, her eyes glistening. 'There seem to have been so many motorbike accidents lately. Did anyone see what happened?'

'No. Only his kelpie, Drum.' Ginny shrugged. 'At least, that's what we assume.' She met Lola's sympathetic gaze and the familiar lump returned deep inside her.

Suddenly, having kept her grief, questions, and thoughts to herself for the past year, sharing them with these kind women seemed the right thing to do. She needed to move forward. Now it was time.

3

*S*he drew a deep breath, assessing the compassionate faces glued to hers.

'He'd gone to shift cattle and was on the way home —we know that because I had to check where the cattle were to confirm his movements to the police. He liked taking the track along the hills above the creek. It was not only quicker but he reckoned he could see everything that way. You know—a good view over the valley and a chance to check there were no animals stuck in the water.' She paused and took a deep breath. 'No one knows what happened next, but it appears he may have hit something as he came out of the cutting. Perhaps his concentration was on the creek and he wasn't looking where he was going. Anyway, the bike rolled down the hill and ... he died.' She sighed. 'When

Drum arrived home without him, barking his head off, I went to find him.' She choked and Lola stood, hastened around the table, and hugged her.

'You don't have to say anything, dear. We understand.'

Ginny shook her head as tears rolled down her face. 'But that's just it. No one understands. Lyndon was so safety conscious. He never rode the bike without his helmet. And he'd had a roll cage built on it for extra safety. Not only that, but they also found nothing on the track that might have caused the roll-over.'

'So, was the helmet smashed to pieces?' Katrina looked puzzled. 'I mean, was it a head injury?'

Ginny looked from one woman to the other. 'He wasn't wearing his helmet. I didn't see him leave, so I can't explain why. And the crazy thing is, we've never found it to know?'

'The helmet you mean?' Katrina asked.

'Yes. The post-mortem revealed he had received a severe blow to the side of his head and was found in the creek where he apparently drowned—despite having been in drought for two years. There was only a trickle of water.'

Katrina inched forward in her chair, her eyes narrowing.

'So there would have been a coroner's inquest?'

Ginny shrugged. 'There was. It was assumed to be an accidental death—but it remains an open case.'

Lola squeezed Ginny's hand again while Katrina sat back in her chair, her eyes wide.

'Wow. I can see why you're so upset. And I thought nothing ever happened in these little out-of-the-way towns.'

Lola huffed. 'You don't know the half of it, my dear. If only these hills could talk, I reckon they'd tell us dozens of stories.'

'Not only the hills,' Ginny added. 'It's times like this I wish our dogs could talk. Drum has certainly been affected by what happened. He wants to go back to the scene at every opportunity.'

'And you?' Katrina asked.

'What, no!' Ginny shook her head vigorously. 'I can't. I haven't been along that track since the police investigation finished.'

Katrina looked down at her watch before standing up and moving around the table. She touched Ginny lightly on the shoulder. 'I'm so sorry for your loss—and I hope I haven't upset you?'

Ginny shot her a brief smile. 'Thanks for listening … it was nice meeting you, Katrina.'

Katrina gave her aunt a kiss on the cheek. 'I'd better get moving or I'll be late getting to the next appointment—and that would never do.' She giggled then, and her pretty, youthful face lifted the heaviness from the air.

'Might see you again next time you're passing through,' Ginny said.

Lola grunted. 'I expect it'll be another few years before this city chick ventures into the country.' She flapped her hands to shoo Katrina out the door before glancing back at Ginny. 'Would you mind packing the lunches into the basket? I'll say goodbye to Katrina, then perhaps you could deliver them to the school on your way home?'

'Of course.' Ginny shot her friend a smile and turned to retrieve the pasties from the warmer.

SHE WAS ALMOST home when she remembered the empty fuel container in the car's rear.

'Bugger. I'll have to get some later in the week.'

As she approached the house, she frowned. Ferocious barking greeted her and her breath hitched at the sight of a brand new Toyota Hilux parked in the yard.

A visitor? Who could that be?

Slamming the car door behind her, she shouted at the dogs. 'That'll do!'

One continued to bark, and she marched toward the kennels. 'I said, that'll do!'

A quick glance around failed to reveal the driver. Ginny lay a calming hand on the roof of Drum's kennel. 'It's okay mate. Shh! Keep quiet now and I'll see who our visitor is.'

The dog quietened, his tail slapping against the timber floor.

Ginny strode to the house, pushed the gate open and leapt as a man appeared from behind a camellia bush.

'Nigel! You startled me.'

Her eyes narrowed at the small, overall-clad figure before her.

'Sorry. I thought you'd be inside but when you didn't answer, I walked around the garden in case you were working somewhere.'

Couldn't you see my car was missing? A memory flickered—a comment made by Lyndon years earlier. 'That neighbour of ours is an odd-bod.'

At the time she had laughed. Nigel was different and she attributed his erratic behaviour to an overprotective mother and the narrow life they led. Despite the constant stream of pickers—mostly backpackers– that came and went on Glenrowan, none stayed more than a few weeks at most and Nigel's circle of friends appeared non-existent.

'What brings you here?' She met his dark, almond shaped eyes, her curiosity piqued.

'It's a year since Lyndon died and I wanted to check you were alright.'

'Thank you Nigel. I'm fine. It's kind of you to ask.'

'If there's anything you need help with, please let me know.'

She nodded, sharing a weak smile. 'Will do.' Her gaze moved to the vehicle in the yard. 'New ute?'

'Yes. Picked it up last week.'

'Lovely. I'm sure it will serve you well.' Ginny stifled a giggle at the vision of the ute bowing to his demands.

'Well. I'd better get back now. I've got a group of travellers coming soon to help get the celery in,' he said.

Ginny nodded. 'Very good.' She opened the gate and stood back, waiting for him to leave.

He raised his felt hat in a brief gesture of farewell then swaggered his way toward the vehicle.

Ginny held a hand up and allowed a fleeting smile to reach her lips despite the wave of sadness that touched her. Good neighbours were gold and yet after twenty five years, she felt she was no closer to knowing Nigel than she did when she and Lyndon married.

She returned to the house, deep in thought. After changing into her farm clothes, she reached for an apple and shoved her wide-brimmed hat firmly on her head.

Reaching the dog kennels, she released Drum from his pen and patted her leg.

'Come on, mate. A whole year has gone and it's time we got a grip on ourselves. Let's go and take another look at that cutting. Perhaps you'll be able to give me some hints, eh—or at least settle our ghosts.'

irk Meyer turned into his driveway on the outskirts of the tiny town of Dalgety and switched off the engine. Slowly extracting himself from the battered LandCruiser, he stared at his home—the one he and Katie had shared for the past fourteen years. The home he and his father had built. His heart was heavy and his hand shook as he locked the vehicle before turning his back on the house and facing the Snowy Mountains.

He had spent his whole life in and around the area, his love of the high country so powerful it was etched into his soul. Now his beautiful wife was buried in the town cemetery only metres from his parents, grandparents, and the tiny, stillborn daughter he and Katie had created so many years before. Friends had been supportive and caring. But their overpowering sympathy was too much. He was suffocating and needed change—to answer the burning need to escape and hide where no one knew who he was.

Unlocking the back door, he strode to the fridge and pulled out a can of beer. He cracked it open and drank thirstily before switching on the television and flopping onto the couch.

Restless and frustrated, he threw the empty can toward the kitchen bin and groaned. Then he stomped into the bedroom, changed into a t-shirt and track pants. He laced his running shoes, picked up his keys, and slammed the door behind him.

The narrow road met the Snowy River Way at the top of the hill and he turned toward Maffra. His breath deepened, and he urged his legs to go faster, harder, while his pulse pounded, echoing in his ears. A white four-wheel drive overtook him as the sign to Black Ridge Road appeared. Turning onto it, he barely altered his pace. An hour later, as the sun dropped behind the hills, he halted, drenched in sweat, and puffing heavily. Slowing to a brisk walk, he turned and headed for home.

For thirty years, his life had been full. He'd turned his hand to anything—construction, maintenance, farm work and even a stint as a park ranger. He'd enjoyed them all. Then they'd been thrown a curve ball, and he had cast employment aside to care for

Katie as she succumbed to the hideous clutches of cancer.

It was time to try something new. With each stride, his resolve grew and by the time he reached home, the only choice still to make was where he should go?

A MONTH LATER, Kirk locked the storage shed in Cooma and made his way back to Dalgety, armed with cleaning equipment and a folder of paperwork. There was nothing more to keep him here and he was itching for change.

The floors were still wet when Trevor, his neighbour arrived.

'Gidday mate. All set to head off, eh?' Trevor said.

Kirk grinned at the middle aged man and sighed. 'I reckon so. I've left the mower in the garden shed, and the basic furniture here in case I change my mind and decide not to come back for a while. If that happens, I'll let you know—and get an agent in Cooma to sort out a tenant. All our personal stuff is now in a storage shed.'

Trevor reached up and rested his hand on Kirk's shoulder. 'Don't you worry about it. We'll look after the place.' He chortled. 'After all, nothin' much else to do here— 'specially with winter just around the corner.'

'Thanks, mate. I appreciate it.'

'Righto. You give yourself a good holiday now. Poke up to somewhere warm and keep in touch.'

'Will do. I'll leave this stuff with you.' He handed the folder of paperwork to Trevor. 'It's just a few bits in case you need them—insurance details, a spare key for the house and the last receipt for the rates. I should be back in two or three months.' He shrugged. 'Or when the snow melts?'

'I'll leave you to it.' Trevor ambled down the drive before giving another wave and turning into his yard.

Kirk returned inside and walked from room to room, checking each cupboard and drawer in case he'd missed packing anything. Surprised when his fingers touched a shoebox in the corner of the main wardrobe, he stood on tiptoes and pulled it toward him.

'How the hell did I miss that?'

Kirk looked down at the box and removed the lid.

His eyes widened, and he grinned to himself. 'Well, well.' He stared at the bag of marbles, and removed the copy of his final school report, gave it a cursory glance, and placed it on the table. After rifling through the handful of photos, their colours faded and blurred, he picked up the small, cloth wrapped package lying on a tattered, hand-drawn map. Turning the parcel over in his long, strong fingers, he carefully unwrapped the irregular shaped rock, coated with dark opaque crystals.

Wrapping his hand around it, Kirk's mind retreated

to his childhood. His paternal grandfather had returned from somewhere in Queensland where, according to Kirk's father, he had been wasting time fossicking. He could still hear his father's roar. *He's supposed to be here, where we can look after him, not roaming around the country!* Too young to understand what that was all about, Kirk had been grateful when the old man had given him the cloth parcel and whispered in his ear, 'One day I'm going back there and I'll be a rich man. You can look after this and come with me when you grow up. It's called Cassiterite. We'll call it tin stone because tin ore is extracted from the crystals.' It had made no sense to Kirk, and his grandfather had died before he was old enough to question him further. But now, with the warmth of the rock safely resting on his palm, snippets of information his grandfather had surreptitiously shared, trickled through his head. A jolt of excitement energised Kirk as he studied the folded map. *Bugger the coast. I'm going to see what Grandfather was talking about.*

With exhilaration buzzing through his veins, he repacked the shoebox, locked the house and walked to his vehicle, laying the cardboard container gently on the passenger seat.

After returning to Cooma, he ducked into the supermarket and gathered a bagful of supplies before returning to the storage shed. He hooked the trailer on behind his vehicle and checked the contents of its lockable boxes—tools in one side, camping equipment and backpack in the other. Then, after connecting the car fridge and transferring the groceries into it, he took a few minutes to run through his list—and drove out of town.

DAYS LATER, Kirk spread the faded, hand-drawn map out on the bonnet of the LandCruiser and studied it. He was close. He had to be. Frustration burned as he followed the web of thin tracks across the fragile paper. Unfamiliar words dotted here and there—nothing that made sense. No *Turtle Ridge*, previously mentioned by his grandfather. Only a cross and a few faint words that resembled *Granite* and *Feather*? Drawn in smudged ink, he knew they meant something—but what? Huffing, he slammed his fist on the map, refolded it and, leaning against the bull-bar, poured himself a cup of coffee from the thermos beside him.

'I might as well give up. I'd be better off heading east to the coast and catch some fish,' he muttered.

A flock of galahs screeched overhead, and he watched them head northward. Then, throwing his dregs on the ground, he tightened the lid of his flask and got back into the vehicle.

'On the other hand—if it's good enough for a bunch of galahs, it's good enough for me.'

Keeping to country roads, he followed signs from Tenterfield, enjoying the scenery and minimal traffic until he crossed into Queensland. The gravel road ended at a bitumen intersection, and he braked abruptly, drumming fingers on the steering wheel. Then, swinging to the left, he followed the road as it wound in and out of valleys, crossed narrow bridges and passed a mixture of bush, alternating with farmland. An hour later, a brown sign edged in white appeared on the roadside declaring he was entering the township of Featherwood Falls, population eighty-seven.

Slowing to the regulation sixty kilometres per hour, his heart leapt with excitement as he cruised along the valley road. *This is it. The town Grandfather spoke of.* A scattering of small holdings morphed to a handful of houses before he reached an old-fashioned two-storey pub, complete with bull nosed roof and wrought-iron balustrade edging the veranda. Drawing to a stop outside it, Kirk glanced across the road at the low set cream building with its sparkling windows, wide timber step and the sign on the roof that read, 'General Store and Post Office'. Further ahead, a Police vehicle sat in a driveway outside yet another historic building, and on the rise overlooking the town, a sign glistened in the late sunshine, depicting a school.

He got out and stretched, noting the tubs of flowers outside buildings and the row of Silky Oak and

Jacaranda trees along the roadside. *A town someone cares about by the looks of things. This is the spot for me—for the moment, anyway.*

OPEN DOUBLE DOORS led into the pub, with a pot of petunias keeping them in place. A mixture of furniture polish and the smell of beer greeted him as he stepped inside the entrance. Uncertain, he hovered. Should he enter the public bar or continue down the hall to where a red and white sign hung above a hatch in the wall? *Office.* A bell sat on the ledge beneath the hatch. But before he could decide, a deep rasping voice sounded from the bar.

'Can I help you?'

Kirk turned into the gloom, his eyes taking a minute to adjust from the brightness of the outside to the dark, timbered walls and floor.

'Gidday. Is it possible to get a room for a night or two?'

A portly man with a bald head and thick grey beard stepped into the light. He stared up at Kirk, as though he was something freshly delivered from Mars.

'It's been a while since anyone stayed, but I don't see why not.' He jerked his head toward the staircase leading off the front entrance. 'D'ya wanna have a look first?'

Kirk nodded. 'Thanks. I'm sure it will be fine.'

As though deaf, the publican gripped the smooth timber handrail and grunted as he took the stairs one at a time, putting both feet on each step before moving up to the next one. By the time they reached the top floor, the old man was wheezing, and he paused, leaning against the landing wall, consumed by a fit of coughing.

Kirk grimaced. 'You okay, mate?'

The coughing stopped, and the old man held out his hand. 'Yeah. Ned's the name. Not too fit these days. Wife blamed the fags.' He burst into another coughing attack, his scalp and portion of face not covered by grey fuzz, turning a deep pink. Kirk waited until Ned regained his composure, a horrified vision of offering mouth to mouth resuscitation flitting through his mind. 'Thought about giving them up so we could grow old together. Then she up and died on me. Heart attack. So in memory of her, I quit.'

Kirk nodded. Did he mean he quit smoking? He assumed so.

'The room?'

'Oh yeah.' Ned pointed down the hall. 'Take your pick. Bathroom's down the end. I'll get downstairs and you let me know what you're doing when you've had a gander.'

'Thanks. I'll find you in the bar?'

'Yep. That's right. News'll be on shortly—not that

there's much you wanna listen to.' He turned and shuffled to the top stair, grasped the handrail again and began lowering himself down, one step at a time.

Kirk raised his eyebrows, took a few steps toward the bathroom, and quietly opened the first room on his right. A small, single bed stood against one wall, covered in a threadbare bedspread. A tiny brown cabinet stood next to it and a dingy wardrobe squeezed between the wall and the door. *Hmm, perhaps not?* He backed out of the room and moved along the hallway, stopping at the last door on his left. In contrast to the dinginess of the first room, afternoon light streamed in from the veranda. A double bed covered with a floral-patterned doona almost filled the interior with barely enough room for the white bedside table and the luggage rack at the end of the bed.

He breathed a sigh of relief and glanced down at his size thirteen boots. *At least my feet won't have to poke into the hallway.* At six foot four, even fitting into a standard double bed was pushing the boundary, but he didn't mind. It looked warm and reasonably comfortable.

Returning downstairs, he wandered into the bar where Ned was idly wiping glasses and watching the television hanging on the wall.

'Beer?' Ned asked.

'Thanks. VB would be great. I'll take the room if that's okay. The one next to the bathroom.'

The old man nodded and plonked a glass and can of VB in front of Kirk. 'Righto. Come far?'

'Sort of. New South Wales. Snowy Mountain area.'

'Oh. Visiting family?'

'No. Just having a look.'

The television blared as the news came on and Ned turned away, leaning his elbows on the bar. A couple of minutes later, he returned his attention to Kirk, as though he suddenly remembered he was there.

'Not much to see around here.'

Kirk grunted. 'I'm following a journey my grandfather took many years ago. Mentioned a place called Turtle Ridge. I was hoping to find it. Explore.'

Surprised at Ned's sudden intake of breath, Kirk met his frozen stare. Ned's eyes had narrowed, and a frown wrinkled the shiny forehead. The older man drew back from the bar, shook his head, and turned away. 'No such place around here.'

Kirk took another mouthful of beer, idly turning the can in his hand.

No such place, eh? Strange reaction. What are you hiding?

5

Stepping out of the farm ute, Ginny shivered despite the midday sun bathing her shoulders. Reaching behind the cab, she unclipped Drum's chain. He leapt off the tray and sat at her feet, his head tilted as though awaiting instructions.

'Come on, then.'

He raced toward the steep track, and she drew a deep breath before striding after him. The kelpie dashed a few metres ahead of her and returned, dropping back to Ginny's pace, his enthusiasm suddenly evaporating.

'Good boy. It's okay. We'll do this together.' She bent and ruffled the dog's ears, meeting his soulful gaze. 'We're on an exploratory project, remember? Let me know if you find anything.' She grinned. *Stupid woman. Talking to the dog as though he's a detective.*

Reluctant to focus on the water below them, Ginny kept to the middle of the track, her eyes straight ahead. Along the top side of the trail, summer storms had gouged a deep gutter in the rocks and gravel and weeds tangled amongst the grey silt. The dry spell had broken soon after Christmas and now the creek ran in a turbulent, noisy rush.

Huffing from exertion, she hesitated as the cutting loomed. She turned her back, absorbing the vista below as she caught her breath. Like a white matchbox toy in the distance, the farm ute was parked nose in to a network of stockyards while a belt of eucalypts hid all but a glimpse of one corner of the homestead, its chimney rising to the sky.

She spun around again and stepped forward, kicking her toe against a rock as she turned.

'Ouch!' She bent to pick it up. Irregular in shape, one side was dark as though freshly broken, while the balance was a soft dove grey. She threw it to the edge of the track, where it lodged against a clump of rough grass.

Frowning, new questions filtered through her mind. What had made it split so perfectly? Were all the rocks black inside? She had never noticed. Squatting again, she retrieved it, rubbing her hand along the darkened side. She sucked in a breath as the sharp edge pierced her skin. A vein of dark crystal etched across the centre of the stone reminded her of something similar she'd seen in the school display cabinet. Wishing she had thought to bring gloves, she continued her inspection. Several lumps of granite had black patches on them, as though having lain buried for years, while others displayed red-brown areas. *Some type of lichen?*

Shaking her head, she shrugged. With the worry of everything else over the past year, the source and composition of gravel was irrelevant. *There's granite everywhere, not to mention every other type of rock imaginable.*

She rested her hands on her hips. 'Well. As far as I can see, there's nothing here those sturdy quad bike tyres wouldn't have driven over.'

Glancing at Drum lying in the middle of the track, watching her every move, she grinned. 'Come on, mate. We'll keep going.'

Treading more carefully, she continued toward the cutting, casting a discerning eye around for anything else that may have caused a distraction for Lyndon. Nothing. Weeds coated the disused track, but apart from that, it looked no different from previous years. Ginny couldn't see anything that might have disturbed her husband's concentration.

Her legs wobbled and she slumped to the ground as memories flooded back. The chunks of earth, ripped from the slope. The battered, upturned quad-bike resting on the ground beside the creek. And her beloved Lyndon lying face down in the water, his head bruised, sandy hair floating in the current. A wave of nausea rose and she bent and rested her head on her knees. Visions of horror, disbelief, and desperation. Tears slid down her cheeks and she hugged herself, rocking back and forth on the grass as sobs wracked her body.

A writhing warmth snuggled under her elbow and she wrapped an arm around Drum, taking comfort in their exchanged sorrow.

She didn't know how long they sat there. Eventually, the sun slid behind a cloud and she shivered. Tipping her head back, she studied the layers of soil and fine stones embedded in the wall of scrub-coated earth. A few metres away, the gigantic split boulder stood proud and solid—its extraordinary division a continuing wonder to all those who passed through it. With impenetrable scrub on the top side and smooth granite falling to a steep slope below, passage around it would have been impossible had it remained whole. Now, a cutting of barely three metres wide provided a perfect alternative for stock to be driven through, significantly reducing the distance between one side of the farm to the other. The steep, green slope below was criss-crossed with narrow sheep tracks forming grey horizontal ripples. And at the foot of the twenty metre grade, the ground evened out for three or four metres before it met the creek bank where signs of previous floods were etched into the surrounding foliage.

Holding Drum's head between her hands, she looked into his eyes. 'If only you could talk.'

The dog turned his head toward the creek and pressed his body against hers.

'I think you saw the bike roll, didn't you?'

She struggled to her feet and continued through the cutting and over the top of the ridge where the land flowed gently toward the neighbouring property. Except for Glenrowan's packing shed and a clump of pine trees hiding the house in the distance, there was no sign of other habitation.

Ginny rubbed her upper arms and focused on the ground for a few minutes. Then she narrowed her eyes, her gaze following the slope to the creek and her mind on the search the police had conducted for the missing helmet.

'I still don't get it.' She shook her head while Drum sniffed the gouged bank and looked back. 'There's no reason for the accident to have happened and no explanation for the helmet. Did he swerve to dodge a kangaroo? Did he see something to distract him?' She released a long, shuddering sigh, remembering the thorough search conducted in the hope of finding the missing helmet, including her own failure to find it in the house or sheds. 'Will we ever know?'

The dog returned to her side and gazed up at her.

'Time to go home. What do you reckon?'

He wagged his tail, and the two of them descended the hill toward the ute.

BARKING ALERTED GINNY TO A VISITOR, and she dropped her dishes into the sink. Peering through the kitchen window, her heart sank. The only burgundy coloured vehicle that frequented Featherwood Station brought nothing but manipulation and angst. She hadn't heard from Lyndon's brother for weeks and silently hoped it would stay that way.

'What do you want?' she whispered.

The gate squeaked, and she met her brother-in-law on the veranda.

'Virginia! How are you? You're looking well.'

Ginny raised her eyebrows, her pulse rising to high alert.

'Thanks Donald. I'm doing okay.' She lifted her gaze to the gate as a car door slammed. 'Is Sarah with you?'

'No. She's busy. Got herself a nice little job with the accountant in town.' His chest lifted, the navy cotton shirt stretching over the belly that seemed to have grown considerably since they'd last met. 'Clever little thing she is. I always knew that, of course—just couldn't be spared from the farm until now.'

'Oh.' Ginny was pleased for her. Having given up a promising career to pander to her husband and son, Sarah had let her dreams of returning to her profession slip at Lyndon's funeral—and on that occasion, listening to Sarah's desires had not been one of Ginny's priorities. 'Please pass on my congratulations.'

The appearance of a gangly teenager broke the awkward moment, and Ginny met his smile.

'Hello Andrew.'

Donald and Sarah's son walked tentatively toward her, bent down, and wrapped his skinny arms around her shoulders.

'Hi Aunty Ginny. Are you okay?' He stepped back, his pale grey eyes filled with empathy. Like his father, he wore jeans and a navy cotton shirt, but that was where the similarity ended. His forehead bore the tell-tale mark of an outdoor worker who spent most of his day wearing a hat and where Donald was broad and overweight, Andrew was tall and as thin as a whipsnake.

Ginny smiled softly at the lad. 'I'm fine, thanks Andrew. What about you?'

'Any chance of a cuppa, Virginia?' Donald interrupted, removing his boots, and pushing past her into the house.

'Of course. Go on in.' Ginny muttered.

Andrew rolled his eyes and grimaced at Ginny. 'Sorry,' he whispered.

She shrugged and beckoned the boy inside.

Filling the kettle first, she set out mugs, took the lid off the cookie jar and removed the milk from the fridge.

'Have a seat.' She waved at the dining table where Donald was already making himself comfortable.

Minutes later, with both hands wrapped around her mug, Ginny gritted her teeth, steeling herself in readiness for what would come next.

'The year's over. You've had plenty of time to think about it ... so what do you reckon?' Donald leaned forward, his elbows on the table.

Before she could answer, he continued. 'You don't want to be struggling here on your own for the rest of your life. I mean, the girls are clearly not interested.'

Ginny opened her mouth to explain that they would be if the world was as it had been a year ago— but she didn't get a chance.

'I've given it a lot of thought and talked it over with Andrew and Sarah. We reckon we could afford to pay you enough to move to town and set yourself up in a nice little house near your mother. Perhaps find a job if you wanted to.' He prattled on, and Ginny closed her ears to his manipulative whine.

How could two brothers be so different? Older by five years, Lyndon had been involved in the farm's running while Donald was at boarding school. Focusing on football and partying rather than his studies or what was happening back at home had always been Donald's priority. A stabbing pain pierced Ginny as she thought of her kind parents-in-law. They had been adamant that Donald have the same opportunities as Lyndon, even if he hadn't appreciated them.

It had been she and Lyndon who had borrowed heavily in order to buy the farm. With the sale of over three hundred hectares on the southern side of the property, they had purchased a second block of land closer to town at Donald and Sarah's request. If it hadn't been for the dreadful car accident that had killed her parents-in-law, perhaps they would have become a united and happy family? But the accident had happened, and it had taken all hers and Lyndon's strength to maintain a civil and fair relationship between the brothers.

'So, what do you think? Andrew's doing well at our place now. Got the gist of cropping down pat, so I'm free to come back here and build up the cattle herd. Perhaps put a manager on so someone's here all the time.'

Something sparked inside her as her gaze met Donald's confident, round face and small, piggy eyes. She pushed her chair back and stood, gripping the edge of the table to still her shaking hands.

'Thank you for your offer, Donald. As discussed a year ago, this farm may have been where you grew up, but you made your choice to not work with Lyndon and I over twenty years ago. Nothing has changed. I have managed for a year on my own and have no intention of selling the property to you or anyone else. It is my home and I will continue according to plans that Lyndon and I made before he died.'

Her legs shook, and she plonked herself back on the chair.

Donald's face reddened while his lip lifted in a sneer. He stood and leaned over the table, his face as close to hers as his belly would allow.

'You'll regret your decision. This is Shepherd's land and it should remain that way.'

Ginny wasn't tall but, having hauled herself to her feet again, she squared her shoulders and met her brother-in-law eye to eye.

"I appreciate your concern for me, Donald ... and for our girls.' She forced a smile on her lips. 'I promise you that if I run into trouble or change my mind, you'll be the first to know.'

She moved to the door and swung it open. 'Give my love to Sarah.'

Refusing to allow Donald to weaken her resolve, she kept a polite smile plastered on her face while he and Andrew pulled on their boots. Andrew leaned down and gave her another peck on the cheek.

'Thanks for the cuppa, Aunty Ginny.'

She patted his arm and followed them to the gate.

In one smooth operation, Donald started the vehicle and accelerated away, a trail of dust in his wake.

It was only after the car turned onto the road that Ginny dropped her arms onto the gate, leaned her chin on them, and waited for the nausea to settle.

6

*C*louds had built in the eastern sky by the time Ginny let the dogs off and loaded them on the back of the ute.

'Ready for a bit of work, team?'

After crossing the paddock behind the woolshed, she stopped in front of the gate and opened it wide, tying it against the fence with a piece of wire. Then, following the fence line, she drove to the southern end of the farm, where Featherwood Station joined Glenrowan.

She swallowed hard. 'I hope you can hear me, love. I know you hated your grandfather selling that land to the Wards, but I reckon I've got more than enough to care for now.'

Turning the ute to face the hill in front of them, she released the dogs and opened the wide double gates.

Bleating greeted her, and she smiled at the raised head of a nearby sheep.

'Hello, Rhea. Have you been waiting for me to come and get you?'

The ewe bleated again, and Ginny spoke quietly to the dogs.

'Go back Chime. Go back Banjo.'

The two kelpies skirted the sheep and raced up the hill to the far end of the paddock. In a flurry, the flock moved toward Ginny and she turned to Drum and Harp.

'Over!'

They flew in the opposite direction to their mates, working the sheep into a swirling cream flock.

'With me, Flute.' The little red dog followed at Ginny's heels, weaving back and forth and never taking her eyes off the sheep.

With reassuring words from Ginny followed by a commanding whistle, the flock of ewes moved toward her, flanked on all sides by kelpies. Then, dropping quietly onto their bellies, the dogs remained motionless as the sheep flowed through the open gateway.

'Good dogs.'

Ginny slid back into the ute and drove ahead of the flock, with Flute running alongside. In quiet control, the dogs kept the sheep in a tight mob while Flute controlled the leaders. Heavily pregnant, the ewes seemed content to continue their journey to the woolshed at a walk. They'd done it all before and Ginny was certain it was because they enjoyed being hand fed and molly-coddled during the weeks before and after lambing.

She grinned at the six ewes leading the flock. All of them had been in the original purchase from a retiring stud farmer she'd met at a sale ten years earlier. Each February, she and Lyndon had attended his on-farm ram sale, gradually strengthening their flock until they registered their own stud. Ginny had studied breeding practices and management, determined to become one of the best and most ethical Dorset studs in Queensland.

'Looks like it'll be triplets again for you this year, Rhea?' she called through the open ute window.

Naming the eight original stud ewes after Goddesses, Rhea remained Ginny's favourite, living up to her namesake as the goddess of fertility and motherhood. She crossed her fingers that this autumn lambing would be less stressful than last years. After Donald's attempt at manipulation, determination burned deep inside her. *I'll prove I'm more than capable of running the place on my own than you could ever be.*

～

GINNY GLANCED OVER THE PADDOCK, confident its gentle contour and plentiful shade and water would provide a peaceful beginning to lambing for the ewes.

At one end of the shed, leading from the paddock, a long, thin addition provided not only shelter from the weather but also allowed portable mesh panels to be assembled to form a row of pens suitable for holding a ewe and her lambs for several days. In between the autumn and spring lambing periods, they could easily be removed to allow access into the woolshed for shearing and crutching of the five hundred Merino wethers that produced the property's primary income—wool.

While the sheep grazed outside, Ginny set to work, carting the panels from under the skillion roof at the side of the shed, and setting them up in a neat row along one inside wall. Allowing an access race on the other side of the pens, she worked until evening, filling each pen with straw, and setting out feed bins and water containers.

Standing at the end of the shed, she rested her hands on her hips and turned to the line of kelpies lying in the fading sunshine.

'A bit more organised than last year, eh, dogs? Come on, time for home.'

All five leapt onto the tray of the ute, and Ginny's heart squeezed. Last year remained a blur, and it had taken months for her to update the records and hope they were correct. Rhea had been first to lamb—on the morning of Lyndon's funeral. For weeks afterwards, sorting out birth dates and checking each lamb was correctly tagged and recorded had been a nightmare. She was determined everything would run smoothly this year, and having Donald help her was the last thing she needed.

As she drove around the shed, she glanced back and frowned. *What?* On the east-facing wall, a sheet of corrugated iron had slipped, exposing a portion of framework. Jamming the brakes on, she leapt out and strode toward it, her frown deepening.

Building maintenance was not her forte. Worse than that, having a secure and well-maintained woolshed was almost more important than the house.

Leaning on the adjacent panel as she wrestled the insecure sheet loose, her stomach sank as it, too, gave way.

Darkness was falling fast. Ginny raced back to the ute and grabbed a torch from the glove compartment. Shining it on the timber, she groaned.

The wood crumbled at her touch and she shuddered at the wriggling white ant-like insects shining in the light.

'Oh no! Termites!'

Her arms dropped to her sides as she recoiled in horror. She stood and stared at the gaping hole for several minutes. A whine reached her from the ute and she turned.

'I suppose I'd better get you lot home and fed.' Her legs felt as heavy as her heart as she trudged to the vehicle.

'There's nothing I can do about it tonight. We'll get on to the problem tomorrow,' she advised the dogs.

A sliver of despair kindled deep inside her as the first drops of rain fell.

Too tired to cook herself a proper meal, Ginny scrambled two eggs and spooned them onto a slice of toast as the phone rang.

She snatched up the receiver. 'Briony?'

'Hello?' The man's voice startled her, and she put her plate on the table and eased slowly into a chair, narrowing her eyes as though to hear more clearly.

'Who's speaking, please?'

'It's Nigel, Ginny.'

'Oh Nigel. I'm sorry. It didn't sound like you. Is everything alright?'

In the seconds of silence, trepidation coursed through her. It had been weeks since she'd spoken to her neighbour but he had now contacted her twice in two days.

Recalling the final conversation she shared with his

mother two years earlier, she twisted her mouth, her heart pounding. The sweet lady had squeezed Ginny's hand, whispering, 'Please keep an eye on Nigel for me? He'll be lonely when I'm gone.' Ginny had reassured her she would, despite Nigel being perfectly capable of taking care of himself. She had been puzzled, though. The Wards had always kept to themselves, even after old Mr Ward died, leaving his wife and son to manage —and they had never asked for help. Why had Mrs Ward been so worried about her perfectly capable son?

'Yes, of course. I've been thinking about our conversation yesterday—and the offer I didn't get to give.'

'Oh?' She hesitated.' And what would that be?'

'If you decide that farming on your own is not for you, let me know. I would be happy to buy Featherwood Station from you.'

Ginny's jaw dropped. *What?* Her stomach did a somersault.

'Thanks Nigel, but that won't be necessary. The girls will both be home soon and I can call on Donald or Andrew if I need anything.'

'I understand. However, it is a large property and too much for you to manage alone. If you're not prepared to sell the whole farm, I'd be happy to purchase the back block.'

Ginny frowned. *Why on earth would he want that part? Suitable only for cattle, it was rough and difficult to access—unless ... of course!* For only a few metres, the corner of Glenrowan touched Featherwood Station boundary—and that portion of land was on a separate title to the rest.

'What would you use it for?'

A heavy, measured breath met her response.

'Same as you. Cattle.'

'Oh! What about the vegetables and fruit?'

He grunted. 'I'm having trouble getting staff with these pandemic restrictions in place—and it's made me rethink my strategy.'

'Fair enough. I'm sorry Nigel. I have no intention of selling any of this property but if I change my mind, I'll let you know.'

Desperate for change of subject, she cleared her throat and plastered a smile on her face.

'How has the harvest been going?'

'We're surviving, considering the circumstances. The celery's being picked now and then I'll get the onions and carrots planted. Apple picking is next—if the workers hang around long enough.' Another pause followed his gloomy response and Ginny toyed with her rapidly cooling meal. Knowing Lyndon's great-grandfather had sold the most fertile part of Featherwood Station to the Ward family had remained both a mystery and cause of frustration. 'What about you?'

'I got the autumn-lambing ewes in today. Won't be long and we'll have paddocks full of newborns.'

'Very well, then. Good luck with your lambing,' he said.

'Thanks. And thanks again for the offer but I'm afraid the answer is a definite no,' she said as kindly as she could. 'Goodnight.'

She tapped the red button and drew a slow breath as Oscar jumped into her lap. Stroking his black coat, she shook her head.

'What's going on, my furry friend? It's a year since Lyndon died and, except for the first few weeks when the place was crawling with police, no-one has offered help until today. Now I've been offered assistance— and have two people wanting to buy Featherwood Falls.' She dug her fork into the scrambled eggs and swallowed a mouthful, barely registering the fact that they were now stone cold.

She snorted. 'Over my dead body.'

7

*K*irk stepped around the sleeping dog and pushed the door open. The bell tinkled, and he breathed in the aroma of hot pies and citrus. *Lemon furniture polish?*

Brushing against a carousel of newspapers and magazines, he paused and picked up a copy each of The Courier Mail and the local paper before strolling across to the array of shelves that lined the side wall.

'Can I help you?'

He looked down at the small, solid woman standing a few metres away and smiled. A blue and white striped apron seemed to cover her entire body and strands of grey hair wafted around her cheery face like a halo.

'Um. Just having a look at the moment, thanks.' He

dropped his shoulders to even their height a little. 'Pies smell good.'

She beamed. 'Fresh out of the oven. Would you like one?'

He nodded and pulled his wallet out of his pocket while she made her way back to the counter.

Handing him the pie in a brown paper bag, she said, 'Haven't seen you here before. Just passing through?'

'Sort of. Having a look around the area first. Maybe hang around and see if I can pick up some work.'

'Ah. There's plenty of that—if you're prepared to do anything.' She held out her hand and then withdrew it quickly. 'Sorry, I keep forgetting we're not supposed to shake hands these days.' She huffed. 'I'm Lola, anyway. Husband's Frank. You probably saw him drive off as you came in.' She waved her arm sideways, almost sweeping the jar of cookies off the counter. 'We run the Post Office here too and Frank does the mail run five days a week.'

Kirk blinked. *Looks like this lady might be just the person I need.* He had returned the friendly wave to the thin, stooped man in a big hat as he pulled up, the action reassuring him that he had landed in a good place. Opening his mouth to speak, the doorbell rang again, and he closed it, turning his head toward the sound.

'Ginny! How are you, love?'

'Hi Lola. I'm back again. Forgot to get the mower fuel the other day.'

'Pump's unlocked. Help yourself.'

Kirk's gaze fastened on the woman. Dressed in jeans and a pale blue shirt, she appeared of similar age to himself and a countrywoman. But it wasn't her clothes that kept his eyes glued to her. It was her face. Framed by shoulder-length, rich brown wavy locks, he wouldn't have called her beautiful—however, something about her smile made his breath hitch. Suddenly aware of Lola's voice, warmth rose up his neck, and he faced the older woman. *What the hell am I thinking?*

'This is Ginny.' She paused for a moment. 'Sorry, I didn't get your name.'

'Kirk. Kirk Meyer. I'd shake hands but, as Lola reminded me, that's a no-go area while this pandemic's around.' His mouth twitched at the corners, and the startled look on Ginny's face softened.

'Nice to meet you, Kirk.'

'Kirk's looking for work, Ginny. Don't suppose you know if Nigel needs more pickers?'

'Sorry. I don't.'

An awkward moment filled the air before Ginny spoke again. 'What sort of work do you do?'

'Pretty much anything. I've got a trailer full of tools with me and have plenty of experience in the building trade or farming.' He shrugged. 'Whatever's needed, really.'

Ginny twisted her mouth and lifted her gaze to the ceiling for a moment. 'Looks like I might need a hand with some building repair work if you're interested?'

Kirk caught Lola's frown out of the corner of his eye.

'What's happened at your place, love?' Lola asked.

Ginny let out a long breath. 'I can't believe it. Termites have got into the woolshed. Just as autumn lambing is about to start and I need it for shelter.'

'How bad?' Kirk stroked his beard. Did he really want to work? He had hoped to get into the bush as soon as possible and explore the area his grandfather had spoken of—that is if he could find it. *Perhaps it's not a bad thing to hang around in here and see what I can find out.*

'I only discovered it late yesterday, but I had a better look this morning. A couple of sheets of iron have fallen off and the timber framework behind them is riddled. The rest look okay but I'll have to get the whole shed sprayed, I guess?'

'Would you like me to have a look at it for you?' Kirk said.

'Sure. I'll fill the jerry can while you eat that.' Ginny pointed to the paper bag in his hand.

'Looks like you don't need me then—except for paying for that lot,' Lola said.

'Of course. I'm sorry for holding you up.' Kirk

fished a twenty-dollar note out of his wallet and handed it to Lola.

While he waited for her to pass the change, his gaze followed Ginny out the front door.

'Here you go.'

He swung back to Lola's wide smile. 'Thanks.'

'Do the right thing by her, and you'll be welcome any time.'

Hurrying to the door, he held it open for Ginny to re-enter. As he closed it behind her, a row of sepia photos and landscapes hanging high on the opposite wall to the groceries caught his eye.

Ambling closer, he squinted and studied them while he bit carefully into the flaky pastry filled with hot savoury mince. Keeping his back to the women, he could feel their curious stares. Pink shame crept up his cheeks and he cursed his emotions while he ate. *What the hell? My poor Katie was only buried a few weeks ago.* He shoved the last of the pie into his mouth, gagging as the rich gravy burned his throat.

'Thanks, Lola.' He heard Ginny say.

Kirk turned, his eyes briefly meeting hers.

He pointed to one of the framed photos as he wiped his beard with a handkerchief. 'Is ... is that Turtle Ridge?'

Ginny's eyes widened, and she glanced at Lola.

'Why do you ask?' Lola rubbed her hands down her apron and moved closer to Kirk.

'My grandfather mentioned it years ago. I'd like to explore while I'm here—that is, if it's possible?'

Lola shook her head. 'As far as I know, it's been called the Camel Hump since before the second world war.' She looked at Ginny, her face solemn. 'It was somewhere up that way that the police did a drug bust a few years ago, wasn't it?'

Ginny frowned. 'Yeah. Over the other side of the ridge.'

'A fella went to jail over it. I know that much.' Lola stared at Kirk again. 'Anyway, you don't want to go anywhere near that place.'

'Can I ask why?'

'You can ask, but I doubt anyone'll tell you. Rumour has it something bad happened there? Something much worse than growing dope. I've lived here for nearly fifty years and I'm still waiting to hear the truth. I reckon you might do well to concentrate on being Mr Fixit and forget about prowling around after ghosts.'

Kirk raised his eyebrows at her dismissive tone. 'I'll remember that. Thanks again.' He strode to the door and opened it, standing back, and waiting for Ginny to pass through. 'Shall I follow you back to your place and have a look at the shed?'

She hesitated for a second, surprise in her eyes. 'Sure.'

He picked up the jerry can of fuel at the same

moment Ginny reached for it and their hands touched. As though an electric shock zapped them both, they jerked back, and he almost dropped the container.

'I'll take it to your car for you.'

'Thanks.' Ginny popped the boot open, then turned back and met Lola's cheeky grin while Kirk stowed the fuel.

Following the silver sedan along the road, Kirk rubbed his beard again, his thoughts a jumble of Turtle Ridge, his grandfather's words, and a strong, attractive, brown-haired woman.

I wouldn't mind betting there are a lot of secrets going on in this place.

8

*A*djusting the rear-vision mirror, Ginny glanced at the mud-coloured LandCruiser in her wake. Behind the windscreen, the new stranger in town appeared to meet her glance, and she quickly dropped her eyes to the road ahead. How could a dark, blue-eyed bearded hunk of a man rattle her so much? And why?

She grunted. Whatever had really brought him to this area was perfect timing for her anyway—even if it was short-lived. If he could fix the woolshed before moving on or getting work elsewhere, it wouldn't matter. The main thing was that she wouldn't have to ask either Donald or Nigel to help.

Parking the car in the shed first, she stepped out as the grumbling diesel pulled up behind her. Her eyes locked on the trailer hooked to the rear of his vehicle.

Metal toolboxes were neatly stowed beneath a bare framework that she assumed capable of carrying lengths of timber, sheets of iron and suchlike.

'Looks like you're well set up.' She inclined her head at the trailer as Kirk slammed the driver's door.

'Try to be. There's always something needed for different jobs, though.' He pointed down the track to the woolshed. 'I presume we head down there and have a look?'

'Please. Do you need your vehicle? Or are you happy to walk?'

'I don't mind walking. We can assess the damage and work out a plan from there. Is that okay with you?'

'Sounds great.' She shot him a quick smile and headed off, his long stride quickly drawing level with hers.

Silently, Ginny stole a sneak peek at the giant of a man. Seasonal fruit and vegetable pickers were common in the area, but for someone other than a backpacker or extended family member to stop and seek work in Featherwood Falls was rare—and puzzling.

'Where do you call home?'

Kirk cleared his throat before answering. 'Snowy Mountain area. A little town called Dalgety. You probably haven't heard of it.'

Ginny grinned. 'Can't say I have, but then I haven't been down that way since I was a child—and about the only thing I can remember was walking to the top of Mt Kosciusko. I must have had plenty of energy in those days.'

He chuckled quietly but said nothing so she continued, her intrigue growing.

'So was it just something your grandfather told you as a child that made you want to stop here?'

Shrugging, he took a few seconds to answer. 'Not only that. I needed to get away for a while and thought I'd poke up and have a look around.'

'Ahh. Camel Hump?'

'Yeah. I asked Ned at the pub but he didn't want to talk about it. Is there something I should know?'

Ginny took a deep breath and squinted, searching the recesses of her memory.

'I know a fair bit of mining went on around here. Mostly tin but some silver and gold were also found— and a few diamonds I believe. You know what the history of mining brings.'

His enquiring eyes met hers.

'Not sure what you mean?'

She shrugged. 'From bits and pieces I've heard over the years, I think prospecting and mining brought more than its fair share of competition and skulduggery—not to mention danger. There's a lot of history around this plateau.' She threw her arm in a wide sweep. 'Featherwood Station was one of the original properties in the area and my husband was a fourth generation farmer. As far as I know, his family wasn't involved in mining, but sadly both his grandparents and parents died early so we never got the chance to hear much about it.'

'Was?' he asked. 'Where is he now?'

Her face softened as a wave of sadness passed over her. 'No, Lyndon was killed in an accident a year ago.'

He pressed his lips together, and his beard quivered. 'I'm sorry for your loss.'

She glanced at him in surprise. The softly spoken words were loaded with emotion—unusual for someone who didn't even know her, she thought.

'Something similar happen to you?'

'Yeah. My wife died recently too—cancer.'

'Oh. My deepest sympathy. Do you have children?'

He shook his head. 'No. We wanted them ... but it didn't happen.'

She glanced at him, a familiar ache spreading within her. *Am I being too nosey?* Deciding not, she continued. 'So now you have nothing to keep you at Dalgety—and you felt it was the right time to move on?'

A fleeting smile touched his eyes. 'You could say that. Good opportunity to do a bit of thinking, anyway.'

They passed the old workers quarters and Kirk paused.

'Do you still use them?'

She stared at the row of rooms opening onto a long

veranda and shook her head. 'Sadly, that was a project Lyndon and I were working on when he died. I haven't had the heart to continue.'

Kirk nodded. 'Perhaps you'll feel up to continuing in time. It looks like it would make great accommodation for farm-stay visitors.'

'Yes—that was our intention. We turned the end room into a bathroom and planned to enclose the opposite end of the veranda for a kitchenette, leaving the middle three rooms for sleeping and living quarters.'

They continued in silence and Ginny led him around the side of the woolshed to where sheets of iron lay on the ground.

'This is it! The latest of my challenges.'

She waited while he ran his hands over the timber and peered through the hole in the wall. Pulling a headlamp from his pocket, he tightened it around his forehead and inspected the ground.

'I can see where they've been tunnelling. Let's have a look inside.'

A lump of dread sat in Ginny's stomach as dollar signs and visions of building noise coinciding with lambing flew through her head. She followed Kirk around the corner and stood beside him as he examined every post and piece of nogging.

'This wall's clean.'

Ginny allowed her shoulders to drop. Biting her lip,

she trailed around the shed as he conducted a thorough investigation. Finally he stood back and shot her a smile.

'The good news is the damage and infestation seems to be contained to this one section. The bad news is that there's evidence of live termites.'

Ginny raised her eyebrows. 'So what do we do?'

'Spray the place with the correct chemical and then set up termite baits. While that takes effect, I'll pull down this section of the wall and replace the framework, then put the iron back on—and hopefully the shed will be good for another century.'

'That's good to hear. When can you get started?'

'Well ...' He stroked his beard again, narrowing his eyes. 'I don't suppose you have any chemical here by any chance?'

'Um. I don't know. If we do, it will be in the storeroom beside the vehicle shed. Shall we go and take a look?'

'Let's do it.'

They strode out, covering the distance more quickly than on the way down, and Ginny's stress levels eased.

Within minutes, Kirk had located a surprisingly new container of chemical that, although opened and partially used, held enough concentrate to deal with the infestation.

'Looks like your husband must have found some elsewhere if this use-by date is anything to go by.'

Ginny shook her head. 'I'm sorry, I don't know. He was very methodical with maintenance so it was something he did regularly and I should have continued. The year has got away on me.'

'Hey, don't beat yourself up. From the look of the place, you've done a pretty good job.' His smile lifted her spirits and her heart did a little flip.

Don't you dare play with my emotions. I've got enough to deal with.

GINNY LOOKED up from the vegetable bed she was weeding as Kirk's vehicle rumbled past the homestead and headed along the track to the woolshed. She glanced at her watch. Ten thirty. The load of cypress timber strapped to the trailers framework indicated he had already followed her instructions to town, an hour's drive away, and sourced the required materials.

While wrestling with the encroaching kikuyu grass, she was torn between the country hospitality instilled in her and the fear of intruding on his apparent preference for solitude. She mulled over whether she should offer to help or leave him to it in case he thought she was interfering. Eventually curiosity won and, at midday, Ginny delivered a thermos, and a small esky containing a meat and salad sandwich, an apple, and a container of biscuits to Kirk.

'I wasn't sure if you had lunch?' She placed the esky on the ground and ran her hands awkwardly down the outside of her jeans.

'Thanks.' His face lit up with a smile and he ducked his head. 'I must admit, Lola's home-made pasties are delicious but having a couple every morning for breakfast is probably not the best health food.'

'Oh? Does Ned not provide breakfast at the pub?'

'Apparently not. He's cooking an evening meal each day which I pay separately for, but otherwise, provisions are my responsibility.'

'Well. I'm happy to provide you with lunch while you're working here—if you're okay with that?'

Kirk allowed his grin to widen. 'Sounds pretty good to me. Thanks again.'

Ginny hovered, resisting a desire to stay. 'I'd better get back.' She gestured vaguely toward the house. 'I'm gardening.'

He nodded in silence and she turned and scurried reluctantly back to the house.

THE PHONE RANG as she was about to deliver Kirk's lunch four days later.

'How's the "Man from Snowy River" getting on?'

'Hi to you too Lola. You'll be pleased to know he's almost finished—and from what I can see, he's done a great job. Certainly taken the weight off my mind anyway.'

'Good, good.'

Seconds of silence followed and Ginny narrowed her eyes.

'Is there something you're not telling me, Lola?'

'Do you think you're safe having him there? Ned thinks there's something odd going on with him.'

'Really! What?'

'Apparently he's been asking questions around town about Turtle Ridge.'

'You mean the Camel Hump? It hasn't been called Turtle Ridge since before the second world war.'

'Yes. I know. It was a mining area but remember the drug plantation up there? Ned seems to think there is something this fella wants to find—maybe he's involved in a drug cartel or there's something hidden in one of the old mines?'

Ginny snorted, choking back a laugh. 'Are you kidding me. You and I both understand that if Ned doesn't know every detail, he makes up a few to make it a better story. I prefer to judge people on how I find them, and not by the opinions of others. And, as far as I am concerned, he has been an efficient and kind worker.' She fanned her flushed face, surprised at how much Lola's comment had rattled her.

'Well. That's alright then. Ned thinks he's too nice to be true and is secretive about his life—so just be careful.' She sniffed. 'I'll get back to sorting out the magazines and let you get on with your day.'

A shard of guilt shot through Ginny. Lola was a long-time caring friend and she squirmed at the abrupt retort she had just delivered. Her voice softened and she smiled as she answered. 'Thanks for ringing, Lola. I appreciate your concern and I promise I'll be careful. Talk again soon.'

'Righto, love. Look after yourself. Bye.'

Ginny put the receiver down, creases deepening on her forehead. Picking up the esky, she wandered onto the veranda, shrugged into her vest, and trod down the track to the woolshed.

'What do you think?' Kirk pointed to the new framework, now re-clad with the original sheets of corrugated iron. 'I've got rid of the damaged timber and will come back in about three weeks to respray if that's okay?'

Ginny smiled. 'That's great. Thanks very much.' She hesitated, the lunch and thermos in her hand. 'I've brought you lunch, but if you've finished, perhaps you'd like to come up to the house instead? We could eat together?'

'Thanks. That would be nice. Before we leave

though, you might want to check you ewes. I think your flock has increased.'

'Really! I walked around them early this morning and didn't think any would lamb today.'

He smiled, wiping his hands on an old towel. 'I'll pack up my tools while you have a look. Give me a yell if you need help.'

Ginny hurried to the paddock, stopping abruptly. She leaned on the fencepost, her face softening with delight. Only metres from her, Rhea was licking a newborn lamb as it struggled to its feet while two others wobbled around her, bunting gently at her stomach in search of a teat.

'You're a clever girl, aren't you? Three babies again.'

She jumped as Kirk appeared beside her. 'Pretty cute, eh?'

'Perfect. She's usually the first to lamb. I'd better put her and her lambs in the shed this afternoon and have a walk around the others.' She pointed to the black clouds building in the east. 'If they decide to drop their load over us later, the last thing these girls need is to be out in it.'

Kirk cleared his throat. 'I'll give you a hand before I leave if you like?'

'Would you? That would be super. I don't like using the dogs with them at this stage and sometimes they're so worried about their lambs they don't realise I'm trying to help them.'

He chuckled. 'I can see you're a sheep lover so I'm not going to comment.'

Without thinking, she slapped him on the arm and laughed, then drew back quickly, sucking in a breath. In a few short days, no matter how hard she tried not to let it, the simplicity and comfort of Kirk's company had grown on her. He seemed easy-going, kind, and helpful. Despite their vastly different appearances, Ginny felt an affinity with him that she had rarely experienced with anyone but her husband.

'Okay. We'll have lunch first, then get the girls sorted.' She turned away to hide her embarrassment and strode back to the woolshed.

'If you wait a second, I'll finish cleaning up here and we can drive to the house together?' he called after her.

Ginny let the breath out she hadn't realised she was holding. 'Righto. Thanks.'

She bent to pick up offcuts of wood and threw them into an empty cardboard carton, acutely aware of Kirk's presence as he transferred the array of equipment into the trailer.

He reached out and took the carton from her. 'Firewood?'

'Yes. Thanks.'

Dropping the box into the trailer, he dusted his hands off, opened the passenger door and smiled at her. 'Your carriage awaits.'

She dipped her head and clamped her lips together as she slid onto the seat, surprised to see how clean and tidy the inside of the vehicle was. She locked her hands together, fingers entwined on her lap.

While he drove along the track to the house, silent questions fought with flashes of anxiety. Suddenly she was tongue-tied.

I think Ned's imagination has run away with him. He's reading Kirk all wrong.

9

*I*nside the familiar kitchen with its polished timber floor and wide gas stove, Ginny regained her confidence as she filled the kettle.

'Tea or coffee?'

'Tea please. Black, no sugar.'

'That's easy. Same as me.' She'd realised after the first day of having the untouched container returned, that he didn't take milk, but, having not asked, had left a small cannister of sugar in the esky.

Over lunch, Ginny strived—as subtly as she could–to delve into her new helper's life. *For peace of mind*, she convinced herself.

'Did you grow up on a property?' she asked.

'Sort of. Nothing like here though. My parents had a small place near Cooma but Dad was a builder by trade, so the farm was more of a hobby than a business. Still, I learned about cattle and sheep—but nothing about operating a sheep stud.'

She grinned. 'It's not too different. Just requires more bookwork and precision when it comes to genetics and husbandry. I prefer animals to commercial vegetable or fruit growing and so did my husband and father-in-law—hence why we've hung onto the merinos in addition to the Dorset stud. When the wool market is up, the stud was considered a bit of a nuisance, but for years, wool prices have been so poor that the Dorsets that have kept this place afloat. Well, that and the cattle I suppose.'

'Don't like cattle?'

'It's not that. I do. We run a couple of hundred here and they're pretty easy to manage. It's just ... well, they were Lyndon's pride and joy and working with them hasn't been the same since he died.'

'So the sheep are your project.'

'Yeah. I guess so. We have three horses as well and when the girls were home, we used them for most of the stockwork—when they weren't at Pony Club and shows.'

'Those are your girls?' He flicked a finger toward the photo hanging above the fireplace—a depiction of a content family of four.

'Yes. It was taken during Claire's final school year. Briony's standing next to her dad and Claire is next to me. Briony lives on the Isle of Skye at the moment with her boyfriend, and Claire's a graphic designer in Sydney. They both came home when Lyndon died but had to return soon afterwards because of their jobs. Since then of course, the pandemic has taken over all our lives and I'm not sure when either of them will get home again.'

'You must miss them.' His voice was soft and understanding.

'I do. Especially at times like this. Which reminds me—it's my turn to ring Claire tonight.' She paused for a few moments. 'The girls and I usually catch up every few days. I'm hoping they'll both manage to come home for Christmas this year ... but who knows?'

Ginny stopped abruptly. What was happening to her? Her plan had been to find out more about this guy, and now she was blabbering the family's life story to him. *I'm not exactly investigator material.*

Kirk drew a deep breath. 'I understand how you must feel. I may not have children, but if I had, I'd want to have them with me as much as possible.'

She studied his face. The shape of his beard indicated a strong jaw beneath, while his tanned skin accentuated bright blue eyes. *Lyndon would have been envious of that curly dark hair.* Her husband had joked about his easy-care style, a thinning cap of fine, tawny hair, and, except for when in the house, he always wore a hat.

Dragging her attention away from the man at her

table, she jumped to her feet and peered out the window. 'We'd better get those sheep under cover. That rain is getting awfully close.'

THE FIRST HEAVY drops splattered on the woolshed roof seconds before Ginny closed the gate behind the last sheep. Grateful for the expanse of roofing installed over the yards years earlier, she and Kirk quickly drafted off the ewes that appeared close to lambing, without anyone getting wet.

Rhea and her triplets were encased in a pen, knee deep in straw, before Ginny gently forced several other ewes showing early signs of being in labour, into an enclosure each.

'Cripes! This is more like a hospital ward than a shearing shed.' Kirk said. 'I guess you're the midwife?'

Ginny grinned. 'Yeah. I don't usually have to help many though and this year, all but ten of them have lambed before.' She removed a hard covered book from its plastic wrap and lay it on a narrow shelf at the end of the row of pens. 'When it comes to studs, correct records and paperwork are as important as the health and safety of mums and babies.'

'Anything else you'd like a hand with?'

'No. Thanks heaps for hanging around. If you hadn't, I would have been out in that, probably swearing at the sheep that stand around sulking when it rains and refuse to move.' She inclined her head to the steady downfall now beating a tattoo on the roof. 'You might want to wait a few minutes until it eases.'

'Will do. Might as well make myself useful in the meantime.' He swung his gaze to the flock contained in the largest yard. 'Where do you want these?'

'They'll be right there until the rain clears. I'll let them into the paddock behind the shed and check them twice a day. That way I can bring in those in labour—and by then, the ones inside should be strong enough to go back outside.'

'How long does that take?'

'Mostly about twenty four hours. But if any have trouble and take a while to mother-up properly, I keep them longer.'

'I'm impressed.' He shot her a fleeting smile. 'What happens if one of them gets into trouble during the night?'

Ginny chuckled. 'If I'm worried, I bring a swag down and sleep here.'

'Bloody hell. That's dedication. I reckon I might come back as one of your sheep in another life.' He laughed then, a deep, rich laugh that sent waves of delight through Ginny.

I don't care what others say about him, I like the man.

'Your bill.' Ginny cleared her throat. 'How do I pay you?'

'Oh that. I'll invoice you—for your farm records. I can drop it in to you some time over the next few days. Will that suit?'

'Perfect.' She shared a smile with him. 'I can't thank you enough for your help. I only hope you're able to get more work ... that is, if you plan on staying around.'

'Yeah. We'll have to see. I'd really like to find this Camel Hump place and have a look. Just wish I knew where it is—and why I'm being warned off?'

Ginny took a deep breath. Access to the area involved trekking and bush-bashing through Featherwood Station—her land. Lola's words echoed in her thoughts. He would have to hang around a bit longer. At least until she'd had time to get to know him better. After all, anyone can put on a good show for a few days. It was when the going got tough that their true colours shone.

She shrugged and stared out into the rain. As suddenly as it had started, the deluge faded and then stopped and Ginny was surprised to see a brilliant rainbow appear. Pointing at it, she glanced at the tall, dark man leaning on the railing a few metres away. 'I reckon that's your sign. Time to head off to wherever it is you need to be.'

He pushed himself upright and nodded. 'I reckon you're right. See you soon—invoice and then to do a re-spray.'

'Sure.'

Ambling away, he stopped and turned. 'By the way. I love your cooking. Thanks again for feeding me.'

She grinned. 'You're welcome,' she called back, running her hands over her curvy hips. 'Can't you see that's my forte?' she muttered.

The grumble of the old diesel engine faded and Ginny turned back to Rhea, shocked at the feeling of emptiness crawling steadily through her.

It was several minutes before her focus adjusted and she bent to check the lambs were feeding properly.

THREE DAYS LATER, Ginny glanced at the pin-pricks of light shining in the pitch black sky. She curled up in her swag on the floor beside the pen housing another of her favourite ewes—one she called Aphrodite. The sheep had been restless all afternoon and Ginny had dashed back and forth from the house numerous times, her concern growing as time passed with no sign of a lamb.

Shortly after eight o'clock, Aphrodite lay down, her breaths short and noisy. Ginny put her book down and scrambled out of the swag. She shone the torch on the sheep's rear, relief flooding through her. A hoof protruded.

'At last Aphrodite. Your baby is coming.'

Ginny unzipped her jacket and threw it onto the swag before rolling up her sleeves. Probing gently, she slid her hand alongside the lamb's leg, feeling for its head. Satisfied it was lying in the correct position, she pulled on the lamb's legs at the same time she felt the ewe's uterus contract. Within seconds, the new life slithered out and landed in the straw. Ginny wiped the mucus from around the little creature's mouth, her excitement fading as it lay there, still, and lifeless.

'No. No. Come on little one. Breathe!' She slapped it's side and blew in its mouth, willing the lamb to show a sign of life. Glancing up at Aphrodite, she realised she hadn't moved either so with a last rub, she lay the lamb back on the straw and moved toward the ewe's head.

'Come on girl. What's going on?'

The sheep blinked and stiffened, startling Ginny. With a grunt and a gurgling sound, Aphrodite moved as another lamb glided onto the straw. Within seconds, it shook it's head and Ginny let out a whoosh of breath.

'Thank goodness.'

There was still no sign of life from the first lamb and she continued to rub it, alternating with sharp puffs of breath into the little mouth—to no avail. She moved the live lamb to the front of Aphrodite, her heart squeezing with love as the ewe bleated softly and began licking her offspring.

Content that mother and baby were safe, Ginny carried the dead lamb to the doorway and lay it on the grass. 'I'll bury you tomorrow, little one.' She washed her hands and arms in the bucket by the door and leaned against the post. In the distance, a set of headlights swept over the land and faced Featherwood Station from the opposite side of the creek. She glanced at her watch and narrowed her eyes. Nine thirty.

'What's a vehicle doing driving around Glenrowan at this time of night?' she muttered to herself. She watched it for a few minutes but the lights went out and she couldn't see anything except the outline of trees that skirted the vegetable fields. Turning back to the dimly lit shed, she chuckled softly. 'Perhaps it's Nigel checking on his vegetable babies—just like I'm checking on my flock.'

Returning to the new mother, Ginny was astounded to see another lamb. 'You clever girl!' The ewe was already on her feet while her third born was shaking his head. He let out a high-pitched bleat and was immediately answered by Aphrodite's deep baa.

Ginny sighed with contentment. It didn't matter how often she witnessed it, the miracle of new life never failed to delight her. She remained beside the ewe for several minutes, glued to the family scene of mother and twins nuzzling her udder. Eventually satiated, the two lambs lay in the straw and Aphrodite lowered herself down beside them. Ginny drew back and returned to her swag.

Switching off the light, she lay on her back, her hands behind her head and a soft smile on her lips. As she listened to the faint grinding of Aphrodite contentedly chewing her cud, all thoughts of mysterious headlights and Glenrowan's vegetables disappeared from her mind.

10

*F*ollowing Aphrodite's delivery, the remainder of the sheep followed suit and the days and nights passed in a blur for Ginny. Tagging and recording new lambs were followed with discharging the strong and bonded families into the paddocks, before bringing in the next draft of about-to-deliver ewes. Then the process was repeated. During Ginny's spare time, she raced around the lawns on the ride-on mower, ran the dogs and tended to poultry, horses—and occasionally, herself.

With only a few ewes still to give birth, Ginny indulged in a long bath and a glass of wine.

'Ahh ... this is the life.' She lay back amongst the bubbles and smiled to herself. *A two hundred per cent lambing! That's a fabulous achievement in any farmer's language.*

With several sets of triplets counter-balancing the number of single lambs, Ginny relaxed. A scream sounded in the distance and her stomach lurched.

'Bloody foxes!' Although it would be foolish to not expect a few losses, the last thing she needed was a rogue fox roaming the place. 'Looks like I'll have to take Flute to the shed with me tonight.'

She sat up and carefully placed her glass on the floor beside the bath. *I wonder if Kirk has a gun license. Perhaps he would be interested in doing a fox prowl for a few nights?* Her heart skipped a beat. Was she wanting to see him again? Or were loneliness and unease over-ruling her common sense.

Oscar meowed, rubbing himself against the bath-room door. He stood, glaring at Ginny as she rose out of the bath.

'I suppose you're annoyed that I haven't been sleeping here to keep you warm?'

She dried and wrapped her warm dressing gown around her. 'Come on then. I'll feed you and stoke the fire. But I've told you before, lambing isn't finished yet —and I can't be everywhere at once.'

Following the cat to the kitchen, she opened the fridge. A half empty tin of pet food sat on one shelf, a few eggs, butter, and a scrap of cheese on another, and the remnants of yesterday's pea and ham soup stood alone at the bottom.

'Hmm. It looks like a day in town for me tomorrow.'

Her gaze shifted to the calendar. 'Cripes. I haven't talked to Mum for days. She'll think I've forgotten her.'

Picking up the phone, she punched in the familiar number and waited.

'Hello, dear. I was about to ring you. Is everything alright?' Mavis White's voice was soft and frail, and concern filled Ginny.

'I'm fine, Mum. Been busy with lambing and I'm sorry I haven't rung you sooner.'

'Oh that's alright, dear. I understand—and I'm sorry I can't help you ... but, well, I think I'd be more of a hindrance than a help.'

Ginny chuckled. 'It's fine, Mum. Thanks though. What's happening—tell me all the news?'

While she listened to the lengthy report of the latest Art Gallery Management meeting, the intricacies of preparing food for Meals on Wheels and the unfortunate fall her neighbour had experienced the week before, she emptied the cat food into the dish on the veranda and topped up the kibble and water.

'What's all that clattering I can hear?' Mavis asked.

'I'm feeding the cats and heating soup for my dinner.'

'Oh! You should be as thin as a rake with the amount of work you do and the little you eat. Do take care of yourself, dear. I worry about you.'

'I'm fine, Mum. I assure you, I'm not starving and I could do with losing a few kilos anyway.'

Mavis tut-tuttered and Ginny rolled her eyes.

'Alright then. I'd better let you go and eat. Talk to you again soon?'

'Of course, Mum. I'll ring you when lambing's finished.'

They said goodbye and hung up, then she poured the hot soup into a bowl, switched on the television, and collapsed on the couch to eat, her thoughts returning to the farm.

'Only a few more days to go—then it'll be the cattle and horses turn,' she muttered.

An hour later, dressed warmly against the chilly night, she returned to the woolshed, Flute at her side, where she found two of the remaining ewes had lambed in her absence—without a hitch.

'Well done ladies. I'll get your babies tagged and recorded and then you can snuggle down and go to sleep.' She grinned at them, relieved the end of her camping in the shed was coming into sight.

She woke with a start, uncertain if the noise she'd heard was real or part of the weird, mixed up dream she'd experienced seconds before—where she was running, stumbling in the dark from something or someone. Taking a deep breath, she held it, listening intently. Wind howled through the trees along the creek, carrying the scream of a fox in the night air. Flute emitted a low rumbling growl, her ears pricked. Silently dragging herself out of the swag, Ginny slipped her coat and boots on and crept along the row of sheep pens. While she'd been sleeping, another ewe had given birth to twins and was standing patiently while her babies tiny heads pushed under her belly, their tails shaking madly as they drank.

Ginny moved to the door and peered into the dark. The night was clear and stars twinkled in its blackness while a cold gust whistled around the corner. She pulled her jacket tighter and zipped it before stepping onto the grass.

Shining the narrow beam of torchlight, she inspected the yards and outside paddock where the older lambs now snuggled against their mothers. A few were standing, but there was nothing to indicate a problem.

Must have been the wind.

She returned to her swag with an uneasiness growing inside her. Chiding herself for her vivid imagination, she shook herself and dismissed her fears—but it was a long time before sleep claimed her.

Around five o'clock, she was woken by a strained baa. In the pitch dark, she wriggled out of bed and turned on the torch. Another sheep was struggling and again, she donned the head torch, rolled up her sleeves and within minutes, had manually delivered a strong, healthy ram lamb.

'Well, no wonder you gave your mother trouble. You're a whopper!'

While Ginny patiently ensured the ewe had bonded and the lamb was feeding, an hour passed quickly, the sky turning a pale, ghostly grey.

She washed her hands and stood in the doorway, breathing in the fresh air, and listening to the birds cheeping as they woke. With the call of nature pressing, she walked briskly around the shed to the outhouse, checking the seat for spiders before she sat down.

It was on her return that she paused, raising her nose in the air like a dog. Something smelt ... odd. Something familiar—and yet, not?

Following the scent, she trod warily in the half dark, using her torch to illuminate her path. Then she found it.

A kerosene tin lay on the ground under the woolshed floorboards, its lid open and a large, wet patch where its contents had soaked into the ground. She recoiled in horror.

'Good God. It's right next to where the sheep and I are!' She whipped around, her heart thumping. 'But who? And why?' With torchlight, she swept the area quickly. There was nothing. No footprints or sign of human life.

The noise in the night. Her head fizzed in alarm. That was it! Splashing. *Someone was going to light a fire —to burn my woolshed down?*

She let out a moan. 'And I was in it with my precious sheep.'

Without returning to check on the ewes, she ran to the house, reaching the gate as a familiar rumble drew near.

Clutching the gate post, she lowered her head onto her arms, panting hard. *So what stopped them?* She angled her gaze to the encroaching sound. Kirk's Land-Cruiser was coming down her driveway.

LONG STRIDES REACHED her in seconds and she studied the concerned face.

'Are you okay? What's the matter?'

She straightened up and swallowed the lump in her throat. 'I'm fine. A bit puffed 'cause I've been running.' With Lola's words still ringing in her head, his early arrival sparked caution and she bit back her fears.

'At this hour in the morning? It's barely daylight.'

'Yeah, I know. Don't worry about me ... what are you doing here so early?'

He reached into his shirt pocket and handed her a folded piece of paper. 'Your invoice. Sorry I haven't dropped it in before now. I managed to get a few weeks work. I'm on my way there now.'

'Great. Where?'

'When I collected the materials for your shed, I left my details with the supplier in case anyone came in looking for help. It turns out a bloke overheard me and rang me soon after I finished here. His wife's stuck in Melbourne helping their daughter or something. Anyway, he wants a new pergola and has a prefabricated summer house he wants me to put together while she's away.'

Ginny raised her eyebrows. 'Crikey. That's a lucky wife. A pretty generous surprise to come home to.'

Kirk grinned, displaying a set of white teeth in the thicket of beard. 'Yeah. Apparently they moved up here just before Covid19 reached Australia. The property isn't big—but it's in a great position. Close to the main road, on a rise with beautiful views and a water course flowing through it. I get the impression money isn't a problem and the farm is one of many assets.'

'Nice. So I guess we won't see you around here much now. Are you still staying at the pub?'

'Yeah. For the moment. This fella's keen to set up a massive garden with facilities to host weddings and stuff. He wants me to hang around and work with a couple of garden designers he's employed ... so it looks like it'll keep me busy for a while and it's not too bad staying with old Ned. Not sure what he thinks of me, but I'm getting used to him and I think he quite likes having someone to whinge about.'

Ginny laughed. 'Oh well, so long as you realise

you're the current topic of conversation and it doesn't worry you?'

'Nah. I'm used to it.'

'Oh.' Ginny opened the invoice, glanced over it, and jerked her head up to meet his gaze. 'Are you sure this is enough? Your charge is very reasonable. No wonder you're in demand.'

'It's fine. I'm not out to make a fortune—so long as the materials are covered and I've got enough to live on, I'm happy.'

Ginny smiled at him. 'I appreciate your help.

'Right, I'd better get on then. Nice seeing you again.' He hesitated for a few moments as though he wanted to say more. 'I haven't forgotten the respray of your shed. Ring me when the sheep are back in the paddock and I'll shoot over and do it for you.'

She nodded. 'Thanks again.'

He was almost at his vehicle when she called out. 'Hey Kirk. What did you do with the damaged timber from the woolshed?'

'I burned it. Chopped it up and lit a fire in the middle of the track.' He frowned. 'I made sure it was well away from the shed and didn't light the fire until you went out somewhere—in case the smoke bothered you. Did I do something wrong?'

'No—it's okay. I just wondered if you needed kerosene to light it?'

He quirked an eyebrow. 'No. It was that dry and

flaky all I used was a match. Why?'

'I found a kerosene tin beside the woolshed and don't remember putting it there—thought perhaps you had and forgot to bring it back to the shed.'

He shook his head. 'Sorry, not me.'

'No worries. Thanks again.'

She watched the LandCruiser rumble down the road, remaining by the gate until the dust had settled. Although her pulse had returned to normal, confusion and turmoil churned within her. Of course she'd seen the dark patch on the road. After all, she had walked past it every day—until the rain came. Then all traces of ash and soot had washed away.

Last night's incident with the kerosene was new—and despite what Ned and Lola believed, she'd bet money it had nothing to do with Kirk.

11

*I*n an attempt to alleviate her worries, Ginny fed the animals and let the dogs out for a run before taking a quick shower. Preparing herself for a trip to town, she took another look at the spartan contents of the fridge and was writing a shopping list when the phone rang.

'Hello?'

'Hi Aunty Ginny. It's Andrew. How are you going?'

Ginny hesitated in surprise. Andrew had never phoned her before—any call from his family was infrequent and almost always from Donald.

'Fine thanks. You?'

'All good. I've finished harvesting the sorghum and wondered if you'd like a hand with lambing?'

Ginny plonked herself in a chair. What? She'd

assumed he thought lambing only occurred during spring—as his father seemed to.

'Thanks for the offer, Andrew. Lambing's almost finished now—only three or four of still to go and everything has gone well.'

'Oh.' He sounded disappointed. Ginny frowned in confusion.

'I didn't realise you were interested in the sheep, Andrew. Otherwise, I would have contacted you.'

'Perhaps next time?'

She took a breath, paused, and released it slowly before answering. 'Sure. We'll see what happens when spring arrives.'

'No worries. Talk again soon.'

'Will do. Bye.' She replaced the receiver in its cradle, racked with confusion.

Why, after over twelve months, would Andrew—or anyone for that matter–suddenly offer help?

Shrugging tiredly, she got to her feet, picked up her shoulder bag and headed outside. She had taken only a few steps toward the gate when she stopped and returned to the house. For the first time, she locked the doors and dropped the key in her bag.

SHE PUSHED the door open and marched into the reception area. The room was silent and she tapped the bell impatiently, determined to make her report before she lost confidence.

From the depths of the living area behind the stations office, a rotund, blue uniformed man in his late fifties ambled toward her, blowing his swollen, red-pocked nose with a dirty handkerchief.

'Ginny! How are you? I heard you've made friends with our new stranger in town—the man from Snowy River.' The officer attempted a choking laugh, followed by a coughing fit and Ginny grimaced.

She and Senior Constable Stan Brennan had never seen eye to eye. After his long-suffering wife left, the local cop had become bitter and his reluctance to do a skerrick more work than absolutely necessary had deteriorated into sheer laziness over the years. Ginny was astounded he managed to keep his job.

'Stan. I need to report something.' She ignored his implication and waited while he tucked the filthy cloth in his pocket.

'Go on.'

His tone was bored but guarded and Ginny fought an urge to roll her eyes.

You're worried you might have to do some work, aren't you? 'I've had a frightening incident happen on the farm and am a little concerned.' Little was not really the operative word, but probably better to underplay her distress, she decided.

'What's on your mind, little lady.'

Heat flushed up her neck at the insult. 'I believe someone has attempted to burn down my woolshed.'

'That's a pretty serious accusation. What evidence do you have?'

'I've been sleeping in the shed as some of my stud ewes have been lambing—and I needed to be on hand for them.'

He laughed and her frustration boiled over. 'Would you prefer I drove to town and reported these issues to your superiors?'

'Now, now. Don't get huffy. It just sounds a bit suss like. You know—sleeping with your sheep? Carry on.'

'Last night I was woken by a noise—but I assumed it was a fox or something, so I ignored it. This morning I found a kerosene tin beside the woolshed with its contents split under the timber floor. I believe the noise I heard might have been someone attempting to set the place on fire.'

She shrank under the man's disbelieving gaze.

'And what evidence do you have?'

'W-well. There's the tin, and the noise I heard—we heard I mean.'

'We?'

'I had one of the dogs with me and she growled. I wonder now if her growl frightened whoever it was, away?'

'Look Ginny. I understand how living alone can make you touchy about things. But, honestly, even if you don't remember leaving the tin there and it was someone else, you may not have noticed it and it only took a fox or a dog to knock it over.'

Ginny's shoulders sagged as anger built inside her. She knew he had no intention of taking her serious and was wasting her time.

'Alright.' She bit her lip. 'I know you don't believe me, but I'd like you to note my concern. After all, isn't that why you're here?'

He raised his eyebrows and chuckled. 'Calm down. You've had a fright, that's all. If it makes you feel better, I'll make a note in my diary that you came to see me. Meanwhile, it sounds as though you need a couple of good night's sleep so I suggest you go home and do just that.'

Without another word, she swivelled and strode out the door. In the car, she counted to twenty before pushing her favourite CD into the player, turning up the volume and setting off on her hour long journey to town. By the time she reached the outskirts, she was calm, resigned and having doubts about her memory. After all, it had been a tough year. She just didn't want to admit she could be wrong.

WITH THE FRIDGE and pantry restocked, Ginny returned to the woolshed to check the sheep. Contentedly grazing while their lambs lay soaking in the afternoon sun, she did a final tour of the nursery.

After removing the soiled straw and topping up the feed bins, she wheeled the barrow toward the door, calling over her shoulder, 'I'll be back to check on you all later.' Determined the new row of trees alongside the track survive frosts and cold winds as winter approached, she heaped straw around each one before returning to the house, slipped off her gumboots and picked up her elastic sided riding boots.

She removed a spider's web from inside one and chuckled. 'Cripes. It's been that long since I rode, has it?' While buckling the chin strap of her riding helmet, she glanced down at Oscar as he wound his way around her legs. 'Go back to sleep, mister. It's not teatime yet.'

In the sun that warmed the steps, the two tabby cats, Sassy, and Kimba, were feigning sleep, and barely glanced at her as she stepped over them. She looked back at Oscar and grinned. 'You need to take a leaf out of your friend's book.'

Minutes later, she scooped a dipper of horse pellets from a heavy timber bin inside the stables, collected a halter, then opened the gate into the horse paddock, rattling the container as she called. 'C'mon!'

Akela cantered toward her, throwing her head, and snorting with enthusiasm, while Rusty and Flash trotted stiffly behind, their destination clearly on the feed bins along the fence in preference to Ginny.

While they each chomped their handful of pellets, Ginny slid the halter over Akela's ears and led her into a yard. Once saddled and bridled, she then led her to the dog kennels and released all five kelpies before mounting with the help of an upturned crate.

Riding along the track behind the house, dogs swarming around the horse and rider brought a leap of joy to Ginny and her smile widened. It's been much too long, she thought.

As they skirted the patch of bush that edged a granite outcrop, a wallaby bounded away and the family of magpies, perched on the branch of a dead tree, warbled as though in welcome. It had been ages since she'd been this way. Except for a quick glance out of the ute window a fortnight earlier, she hadn't checked the steers for weeks and guilt surged inside her. *Lyndon would be horrified.* She reassured herself that in many areas of Queensland, cattle went months without seeing a human—and they survived, didn't they? Anyway, Featherwood Station had plenty of feed, good, solid fences and an automatic watering system that kept the troughs full. The cows were closer to home and easier to check. Anyway, none were due to calve until spring—so what was there to worry about?

Akela jogged, swinging her hindquarters, and spooking at imaginary ghosts in the bush.

'I can see you need a lot more exercise than you're getting, my girl!' Ginny stood in her stirrups and rubbed her aching back. 'And I reckon I might need the same.' She grinned ruefully and patted the horse's neck. 'Settle down. You'll be too worn out to walk home at this rate.'

After checking on the troughs in the cow paddock, Ginny nodded contentedly. Grazing amongst the scrub, she noted the stock looked healthy, the feed level holding well and there would be no need to move them for a while yet.

Continuing up the range, she rounded a clump of boulders on the crest of a hill and drew rein, taking a few minutes to absorb the vista in front of her. Swathes of tawny coloured grass waved in the breeze, morphing to the smooth green valley where cattle gathered in one corner. The windmill stood silent, and Ginny squinted at the gathered herd. A sea of Black Angus milled lethargically, their bellows reaching her despite the wind.

She felt the blood drain from her face. 'Something's wrong.'

Gathering her reins, Ginny urged Akela into a trot and they scrambled down the hill to where the ground opened up and she could increase their pace. The horse leapt into a canter at Ginny's command, her rider's pulse thumping in rhythm with Akela's hoof beats.

As she drew near, Ginny sucked in a horrified breath and groaned. The steers were sluggish, their flanks hollow when they should have been fatter than the cows. She rode along the fence line, noting the handful of youngsters that had leapt the fence and were grazing contentedly beside the creek in the adjacent paddock. Sliding off Akela, she tied the mare to a fence post and walked toward the mob.

'The windmill's not pumping?' Ginny spoke allowed, as though to reassure herself of the diagnosis. Her step lengthened and she picked up a stick, waving it in front of her to prevent the massive bovines from knocking her to the ground.

'Bloody hell.' She tipped her head back, studying the silent rods that should have been plunging up and down, drawing water and spilling it into the long, concrete trough that sat perpendicular to the windmill. The lever engaging the rods was hooked on the supporting frame of the blades—and tied with wire so that no matter how hard the wind blew, the rods would not be able to move.

In a trance, Ginny walked around the structure, wracking her brains. With no water drawn from the water table beneath the ground, the trough was bone dry. How long had it been like that? She reached up and unwound the wire before releasing the lever. The gigantic blades caught in the wind immediately and swung, creaking, and moaning as they began to rotate.

Holding her breath, Ginny watched, her fingers crossed and her heart pounding. To her, it seemed like hours, but within a couple of minutes, a trickle of water flowed out of the pipe and ran into the trough. Several beasts rushed forward, licking the concrete as it flowed.

How did it get like that? Ginny waited, watching the water flow, her legs shaking as she registered the possibilities. 'I know that I did not turn it off.' She spoke to the cattle apologetically, as though they understood every word.

Following the overflow pipe along the fence, she reassured herself it was still connected correctly, allowing any excess to trickle into the creek. Everything appeared untouched. Continuing further down the paddock, she threw open the gate and whistled the dogs, guiding them around the escaped cattle with a series of commands.

Minutes later, with the escapees back in the correct paddock with their mates and the water flowing evenly into the trough, Ginny remounted Akela. Hovering nearby, she waited until she was sure all cattle had drunk their fill before turning for home.

Bile filled the back of her throat and she looked down, surprised to see her hands shaking.

Someone did this. Why? To frighten me. To make me rethink selling. Or something more sinister.

Without hesitation, Akela broke into a canter and

with the dogs running alongside, they returned to the homestead in half the time it had taken to ride out.

Ginny rubbed her temples in an attempt to quell the rising pain. After brushing the horse down, she released her back into the paddock and shut the kelpies in their kennels. Then she marched to the house and picked up the phone.

'Hello?'

'Stan? Hi, it's Ginny Shepherd.'

'Again? What seems to be the problem this time?'

Ginny drew a deep breath, determined to keep her cool and then poured out her concerns about the interference with the windmill.

'I was lucky none of them died.' She finished indignantly.

'Righto. I get your point. Are you sure you didn't forget to engage the gear last time you checked the mill?'

'Yes, totally sure. I had to grease it during summer and I don't know if it's a job you're familiar with, but if you were, you would know that involves ensuring it pumps smoothly afterwards. I did that—and I know I didn't leave until I was sure water was flowing freely. That CAN'T happen if the lever has been disengaged.'

'Okay. I'll come for a drive tomorrow and have a look for you. Meanwhile, perhaps you should think again before you get that fella back on your farm.'

It took Ginny a few seconds to realise he was

talking about Kirk. Fury built again but this time she bit her tongue.

'Is there something I should know about?'

'No, no. I'm just keeping my eye on him. You never know with strangers.'

'I see. Thank you. I'll see you some time tomorrow.'

Before she replaced the receiver, a chuckle echoed down the line. Slamming the phone down, she raced to the bathroom and splashed cold water over her face to quell the burning fury.

12

*H*aving decided an early night in her own bed was needed, a phone call from Claire in lieu of watching television could not have been more welcome.

'Hello?'

'Mum! It's me, Claire.'

'Hi darling. It's good to hear from you.'

'Are you okay? Your voice sounds funny.'

'I'm fine. In bed though so perhaps it's the phone?' The last thing Ginny wanted was for either of her girls to be worried about her.

'What are you doing in bed at this hour? It's only seven thirty!'

'I know. I'm tired, that's all. Autumn lambing has finished—except for a couple that are a bit late. Because last year's records ended up being such a mess, I decided to sleep in the shed and keep up with the tagging and recording as each ewe gave birth.'

'Good grief! Do you mean you've been sleeping in the woolshed?'

Ginny chuckled. 'Yes—I know, you think I'm mad. Well, join the club. Anyway, it's been very successful and the bookwork is up to date. I'm a bit tired though so decided to have an early night.'

'Good on you.'

Desperate to divert the attention away from herself, Ginny spoke before Claire could ask any more. 'What's the weather doing down there? And how's work?'

'It's sunny but getting quite cool now—winter is on its way. And work is fine. I've been given two new projects and am quite chuffed. Both are for big companies and they specifically asked for me.'

'That's wonderful, darling. What are you designing?'

'One company is updating their logo—so I'm not quite sure where that will lead. Maybe nothing? But the other wants me to redesign everything. Brochures, logo, business cards—the lot.'

'I'm very proud of you and pleased that your study is paying off. Achieving a good name as a Graphic Designer will always stand you in good stead. What about your social life? Have you been able to get out and about much?'

A loud huff whooshed through the line.

'Huh. You've got to be joking. The restrictions are so tough at the moment it's hard to go anywhere. Except for a run and a bike ride each day, I hardly see anyone. On the positive side though, I am able to connect with my friends through our online chat group—and we've been playing a few games online which are fun.'

Ginny raised her eyebrows at the thought. Online games and chat groups were part of another world for her—and she didn't attempt to ask for an explanation.

'Have you heard from Briony?' Claire asked.

'Not for a few days. She left a message on the answerphone to say all was well though. I'll try to call her tomorrow. I think she's decided to stay in Scotland for the summer but hopefully she'll be able to come home for Christmas.'

'I talked to her on What's App last week. She and Alex had the day off and were heading off for a hike in the Cuillin Mountains. Apparently the weather has been gorgeous over there. I think they're as fed up with restrictions as we are and were bursting to get out and about. I can't imagine them meeting too many people in the Cuillins though so social distancing won't be a problem.'

'That sounds lovely. I do understand how tough it's been for you all. Sometimes I feel like a hermit here, but in times like this, I'm pleased I live in such a gorgeous area and have so much space to roam around in.'

'How are the horses? Are you riding them?'

Ginny swallowed her guilt. The girls had been adamant that she ride regularly—for her own benefit as much as the horses, and with the exception of today's ride, she hadn't been on a horse for weeks. 'I rode Akela today to check on the cattle, but the boys haven't had a ride for a while. I didn't think they needed unnecessary exercise. Poor old Rusty is starting to show his age and Flash is not far behind. I bought them some of those gummy nuts when I was in town today to help them stay in good order through winter.'

'Great. Well, I'd better sign off now, Mum. I've got a zoom meeting starting in five minutes.'

'Okay. Thanks for ringing. Love you.'

'Love you too, Mum.'

Ginny stared at the phone before replacing it in the cradle. *What the hell is a zoom meeting? One that is short?* She presumed so.

Snuggling down under the doona, Ginny listened to the wind in the stand of gumtrees behind the house and reflected on her day. On one hand, she was relieved Claire hadn't cross-questioned her about the cattle, but on the other, her anxiety heightened. Could it really be Kirk doing this to her? She pulled the pillow around her ears. Of course not. He was unfamiliar with the area and certainly wouldn't have any idea where the boundaries of Featherwood Station were—or who owned the windmill. It had to be someone who knew her. But why? What had she done to deserve this?

It was a long time before sleep claimed her, despite her physical exhaustion.

THE FOLLOWING morning dawned bright and crisp— one of those early winter mornings that makes a person feel alive. Ginny rose early, checked on the sheep, fed the horses and chooks, and took the dogs to the waterfall for a walk. Although Stan hadn't committed to a time, she was sure he would turn up when she least expected it—and there was no way she would allow him to return to town with the excuse *she hadn't been there so he couldn't follow up her complaint.*

Back in the house before eight, she dragged the vacuum cleaner from the cupboard and spent most of the morning, cleaning and tidying the house. She swirled the broom around the high ceilings, astonished at the number of spiders and amount of dust that had accumulated in what she believed was a very short time—considering there was only one person living in the house.

With a quick trip down to the woolshed at lunchtime, she reassured herself that all mums and babies were safe and happy, while her eyes and ears remained tuned to the road. The afternoon dragged, the sun spreading a soft golden glow across the ridge behind the farm before the white Toyota with the blue trim and bar-light on its roof eventually arrived at the gate.

Ginny hovered in the yard while Stan took his time extracting himself from the vehicle, his belly bursting over the top of a low-slung belt.

'Gidday.' He slapped a wide brimmed felt hat on his balding head and ambled toward her.

'Thanks for coming Stan. Would you like to go straight to the woolshed—or out to the windmill first?' she said briskly.

'How about we head out to the paddock first in case darkness catches us out.'

Ginny nodded and pointed to his vehicle. 'You want to drive? Or will we take my ute?'

'I'll drive. You can do the gates.'

Of course—why didn't I think of that. She bit the words back, determined to keep her irritation in check. *I will not let this man rub me up the wrong way.*

She held the dash handle tightly, rocked from side to side as Stan bounced the vehicle across the paddocks. His disregard for anything but the largest of rocks in his path astounded Ginny. *Now I know why QPS allocates a new vehicle to him every couple of years.*

Their destination revealed cattle spread across the

paddock grazing and Ginny breathed a sigh of relief. She jumped out of the wagon and swung the gate open. Stan drove through, and her gaze swept the stock, reviewing their condition as she fastened the latch. Thankfully, the hollowed flanks had already filled and lasting effects of depravation appeared to have been avoided.

'This is the windmill you reckon was tampered with?'

'Yes.' She reached for the piece of wire looped around one leg of the mill. 'If you have a close look, you'll see the wire has lots of kinks in it where it was wound around the lever and attached to the frame, preventing the blades from turning.'

'And you reckon you didn't switch it off or put the wire around it.'

'Of course not. This is the only water source for this paddock. I'm not stupid.' She spat the words without thinking.

'Okay. Settle down.' He grinned. 'You're a bit feisty, aren't you?'

Ginny took a deep breath and gritted her teeth. Lowering her tone, she answered as pleasantly as she could. 'I assure you, Stan. I am not feisty. However I am both worried and a little frightened. It may seem like a joke to you, and I know I don't have much evidence— but to me, it appears as though someone is trying to frighten me. I am relying on you for guidance here.'

He lifted his hat and scratched his head, squinting closely at the piece of wire. 'Okay. I'll take a few photos.' She glanced down at the full body of water rippling in the evening breeze. Yesterday, it had been a dry concrete bed and the cattle desperately thirsty. Now—she was no further ahead and it didn't appear that Stan was going to be much help.

'It's a shame you didn't think to take photos yesterday when you found this.' He snapped several shots with his smart phone as he wandered around the windmill.

'I never thought of it. As you know, there's no mobile coverage in the area so I rarely carry my phone with me unless I'm going to town.'

'Of course.' A glimmer of a smile touched his ruddy face. 'I suppose you're like me, rely on the land-line if you want to talk to anyone.'

'Hmm. Shall we head to the woolshed now—before it gets dark?'

'Righto. Jump in.'

She hurried to the troop carrier and fastened her seatbelt while Stan grunted his way into the driver's seat.

Passing the homestead, Ginny directed Stan straight to the woolshed. He handed her a torch, pulled a head-lamp over his forehead, and followed her before the light faded completely. First snapping shots of the dark, damp ground under the edge of the shed, he then reached down and ran his fingers over the ground. He rubbed them together, sniffed them and stared at Ginny with raised eyebrows.

'You could be right. It certainly smells and looks like kerosene has been spilt. A typical four litre tin probably sits in most people's sheds around here. Is it yours?'

'I'm not sure. We did have one in the work shed and I checked—it's not there now. But I don't know how it would have got here. So, you agree I should be concerned?'

'Is it possible that Lyndon left it here and you haven't noticed it until now?' Stan asked.

'Why would he do that?'

'Well, you mentioned you've had a termite prob-lem. Perhaps he was planning to use it on the nest?'

She shrugged. 'I don't know. He didn't mention anything to me—and I'm sure I would have seen it before now.'

'I see there's tyre tracks here. Are they yours?

'No. They'd be Kirk's. He repaired the termite damage to the shed for me recently.'

'Could he have put the tin here?'

A sudden vision of Kirk's vehicle parked close to the wall, enabling him to stand on the back of it instead of using trestles sprang to mind. She hesitated.'

'I don't think so—but I haven't asked him.'

'You don't think so. But you can't be sure.'

'No.'

'It does seem fresh—but I suggest you have a talk to him. I reckon you'll find your answer there. He probably left it and one of your dogs has knocked it over.'

She faltered, frustration growing as the shadow of doubt reappeared. 'So that's it? You want me to talk to Kirk and you don't think it's worth investigating?'

'Not at this stage. There's simply not enough evidence. Tell you what—give me a call if anything else bothers you and I'll pop back again for a talk.'

Ginny bit back a groan. 'I will.' She crossed her fingers in the dark. *I dearly hope that won't be necessary.*

13

A week later, Ginny moved the ewes and lambs to new pastures on the northern side of the house—the warmest area for young lambs as winter crept in–and close to the house for her to review them regularly.

She checked the farm diaries for the past three years, scrolling through the regular chores that Lyndon had carefully recorded. The previous year was blank— her fault. Her head had been in a fog and remembering to keep the diary up to date hadn't crossed her mind. Sending a quick prayer to her husband, she thanked him for his diligence. It was certainly helping her now and she dutifully noted the past week's activities and double-checked she hadn't missed a week.

Her fingers rested on the last week of June, two

years earlier, where the words, *preg test cows*, was written in Lyndon's neat, round hand-writing.

'Bugger. I forgot about that.' She stared through the window and frowned. A sharp wind whipped across the yard, scattering the last of the leaves from the Crimson Spires.

Rising from the office chair, she stoked the fire and paused to rub Oscar's ears as he lay stretched out on the hearth rug. Sassy and Kimba curled in a tangle of tabby limbs on the cat bed nearby, and on the veranda, Flute's head was barely visible, resting on the edge of the new, soft dog bed Ginny had bought her.

She rubbed her upper arms and sighed. 'Not a particularly nice day to be sorting cattle but I guess it's not going to get better—for a few months anyway.'

He mind flicked to the tall, dark man from the Snowys and she pursed her lips, remembering the note he had left on the door advising he hadn't forgotten about respraying the woolshed and would be back. She wondered if she should ring him—ask if he could help with the cattle work? Her stomach did a little dance, surprising her. 'A cuppa is what I need, not a man—except the vet of course.'

The following day dawned still and icy cold, freezing the water in the bird bath and dogs containers.

Ginny wound her scarf more tightly around her neck as she fed the chooks and let the dogs out. Expecting to have to wait at least a week for a vet, she had been flustered when the receptionist announced Jeremy would be at her place by nine o'clock the following morning. However, it was a job that had to be done, and the sooner, the better.

'C'mon!' She called the horses as weak sunshine melted over the hills to the east. As always, Akela was first to arrive and Ginny quickly locked her in a stall before the two older horses arrived at an arthritic trot. She straightened their rugs as they ate and then saddled Akela.

'We've got a bit of work to do, my girl.' Akela peeled her lips back, dropping pellets on the ground and stamped a hoof. Ginny laughed as she pulled on gloves and helmet, then led the mare outside, mounted and turned her southwards.

Covering the distance at a brisk trot, Ginny paused only to open gates and prepare the cattle yards for drafting. When she reached the hundred hectare paddock where the cows had been for the past few weeks, she whistled the dogs. One by one, she gave them commands, then waited as they raced along the fences toward the back of the paddock.

Standing well back from the gate, she counted the lumbering black beasts as they trotted onto the track and turned toward the yards, breathing a sigh of relief when the hundred and fortieth cow passed through.

'That's the lot. Good dogs!' she called.

Steadying the herd to a walk, she trailed behind them while the kelpies flanked each side. In her usual position, Flute trotted before them, ensuring none overtook her or attempted to break away.

Ginny glanced at her watch and grimaced at the dirty vehicle parked beside the yards.

'Bugger. Just the day I would have been happy for you to be late, you're early,' she muttered. Giving the vet a welcoming wave first, she then concentrated on ensuring all cows were in the holding yard before dismounting and closing the gate. She led Akela to a spare yard and unsaddled her. The mare lowered her head and nibbled the fresh shoots of grass that had pushed their way around the edges. Alongside them, a belt of massive Casuarina trees protected the yards from the western sun and cold southerly winds.

'Gidday, Jeremy. Thanks for coming out so quickly.' She shot a smile at the young, auburn haired vet.

'No worries. We've got a couple of vet students with us at the moment so Sonia is supervising them for the morning clinic.' He shrugged his wiry body into a pair of dark green overalls and rolled up his sleeves. 'Right. Let's get these girls into the race.'

He donned a pair of shoulder-length surgical gloves, shouldered the battery operated ultrasound scanner onto his back and fastened the headpiece over his forehead. Meanwhile Ginny and the dogs pushed the first few cows into the small yard, funnelling them up the race and into the crush.

'Ready?' she called.

He nodded and picked up the ultrasound wand.

Working methodically, Jeremy examined each cow before calling the results to Ginny, while she scribbled the information in her pocket diary and ran back and forth, releasing each cow from the head bail and pushing the next one into place.

It was midday before they paused for a break and Ginny blew a long sigh of relief.

'Not too bad so far.' She grinned. 'Over half way through and only a handful of empties. Would you like to nip down to the house for a bite of lunch before we continue?'

'Sounds great. Thanks.' Jeremy stripped off his gloves and gear while Ginny tied the dogs up beneath the trees.

AN HOUR LATER, satiated by Ginny's pea and ham soup and freshly baked bread, the sound of a vehicle approaching startled her.

Annoyed that today of all days, she was too busy to

stop to socialise, she shot an apologetic glance at Jeremy.

'Sorry. I won't be a minute. Enjoy your coffee and I'll be back in a tick.'

He grinned and reached for an apple from the fruit bowl on the table. 'No hurry.'

Rushing down the steps, Ginny opened the gate and stared, her eyebrows rising as Andrew stepped out of the low slung blue utility.

'Hi Aunty Ginny. How're things?'

Ginny quavered. Since when had Andrew ever popped in randomly to say hello?

'Hello, Andrew. Everything's fine thanks. What brings you out here today?' she asked brightly, hiding her apprehension.

'Dad said it would be about time to get the cows preg tested and I thought you might like a hand.' He turned toward the ute and gave a shy grin. 'And I wanted to show you my latest acquisition.'

She cast a glance over the sparkling, bright blue Commodore utility.

'Very nice.'

His grin widened. 'Yeah. One of the last to be manufactured in Australia. Should be worth a bit in a few years.'

Sure, if it lasts that long—or will Daddy buy you something nicer by then? Ginny returned his smile, squirming with embarrassment at her thoughts.

'We're having lunch at the moment. Would you like to join us?'

'Thanks.' He frowned. 'Who's we?'

'You'll be pleased to hear it's the vet—and we're over half way through testing the cows now.'

'Oh.' His eyes widened and he followed her silently back to the house.

'Jeremy, this is Lyndon's nephew, Andrew.' She waited while they chuckled.

'We know one another.' Jeremy explained. 'I look after Donald's cattle too.'

Ginny bit her lip as irritation rose inside her. 'Of course. I should have known that.' *So why are you coming to check on me. Did your father check with the clinic before he sent you here?*

She ladled soup into a bowl and placed it in front of the young man.

'Tea or coffee?'

'Coffee please.'

Ginny glanced at the clock, her heart pounding. She wasn't sure why she allowed exasperation to consume her. Of course Andrew could have helped. But, having not made any attempt to assist the previous year when she had needed it so badly, she no longer trusted either Donald—or Andrew, no matter how pleasant the teenager appeared.

While the men dawdled over lunch, Ginny excused herself and went to the bathroom. Leaning on the basin, she studied the reflection in the mirror. She touched a strand of grey amongst the wavy brown hair that escaped its tie and gazed into the hazel eyes, shadowed by dark rings. Fine lines had appeared on either side of her mouth and she held her palms against them as sadness engulfed her.

Lyndon, why did you have to leave me? We were supposed to grow old together.

Shock sparked her and she stood up straight. It wasn't Lyndon's face that flickered through her mind, but one of a dark bearded man with kind, blue eyes.

Splashing cold water on her face, she turned and grabbed the hand towel, shifting her gaze away from the mirror.

What am I thinking? She hurried back to the living room.

'Are you ready to get back to it Jeremy? The days are getting short and I'm not keen on finishing up in the dark.' She added a smile to soften her comment.

'I'll hang around and give you a hand.'

'Thanks Andrew.' Ginny's answer was weak, her energy waning rapidly.

AS EXPECTED, having an extra pair of hands hastened the job enormously. With Andrew pushing the cows up in quick succession, Ginny operated the head bail, and recorded each cow's number and stage of pregnancy.

By late afternoon, the job was complete and twenty four cows stood in one yard while the balance filtered into the paddock surrounding the yards.

'I'll be off then, Ginny.' Jeremy closed the back door of his wagon and slid into the driver's seat.

'Thanks again Jeremy. Bye.' Ginny gave him a wave and turned to face Andrew. 'I'll be okay here now. Thanks for your help.'

'Let me give you a hand to get these into their respective paddocks before I go.' He looked at the empty cows in the yard. 'Where do you want this mob put?'

'They can go in the dam paddock below the ridge with the bulls. I'll take those in calf to the big hill on the other side. There's stacks of feed there and plenty of shelter so they should be okay until spring.' She waved an arm in the opposite direction from where they'd been grazing earlier that morning.

'Righto. I'll wait until you get your lot out of sight and then move these girls.'

Ginny shot him a grateful smile and resaddled Akela. Weariness filtered into every limb and she struggled to mount the patient mare.

'Come on girl. One last job for the day then we can go home and relax.' She turned to Andrew and smiled. 'Thanks again Andrew. Don't wait for us to return—

we'll take a lot longer than you will and you'll want to get on the road before the kangaroos do!'

He grinned and gave a mock salute. 'Sure will. See you next time.'

'Bye.' She whistled the dogs and followed the herd along the track, pausing while the cows snatched mouthfuls of grass. The last rays of the golden orb sank behind the ridge as Ginny latched the gate and turned for home. Birds twittered as they nestled in for the night and the temperature dropped.

Ginny turned her collar up and slid a hand into her pocket. A soft frown formed between her eyes.

How had Donald known she would be working with the cattle today? Had he really sent Andrew to help—or was there an ulterior motive?

14

*K*irk straightened and stood back to admire their work. Following the erection of the summer house, he had spent a week constructing the pergola. It had taken another three days to paint it, with both he and Neil, the owner, working every daylight hour they could. Tomorrow, Neil's wife, Valerie was due home and Kirk knew he wasn't the only one looking forward to a couple of restful days.

The estimated "week or two" of work had stretched out to over a month and now Kirk's mind rested on his own situation.

After gathering his gear and loading the trailer, he waved goodbye to Neil and headed back to his tiny room at the pub. Chewing over Neil's final request, he wondered if he would regret his decision. With grand plans for the events facility to be completed by the time the world returned to normal, Neil's enthusiasm was contagious and Kirk had accepted his offer of continued work without thinking.

Now, a face with an attractive smile and soft brown hair filtered into his thoughts and his stomach fizzed with anxiety. He had only been at Neil's property, newly named 'Kallala', for two weeks when he had called at Featherwood Station on the way home, hoping to see Ginny and to give her woolshed a second termite spray. He had knocked on her door to no avail, and, noting the vehicles were still in the shed, presumed she had gone for a ride. With darkness closing in, he had left a note tucked into the flyscreen door, advising he would be back to complete a thorough job within a week or two—and now, that promise was well and truly overdue.

'It looks like it's time to make a few more decisions,' he muttered to himself.

Driving into the pub carpark, he parked against the back fence and locked the vehicle, heaving a loud sigh. The store was shut for the night and he was tired of Ned's repetitive menu. Beef casserole and spuds on Monday's, Wednesday's and Friday's, steak, chips and salad on Tuesday's, Thursday's and Saturday's, and a pork roast on Sunday's. They were tasty and hearty, but he longed for a piece of fish or a tangy stir-fry. Still, he supposed at least he could get a meal. There were plenty of pubs and cafes that had been forced to close indefinitely.

His new friendship with Neil brought with it a reluctance to leave the area—for now. The weeks in Featherwood Falls had disappeared in a flash, and a wave of panic washed over him. *I haven't even begun to follow up Grandfather's discovery!*

That evening, Kirk wolfed down his dinner while the grumpy, reticent Ned complained about the government, the pandemic, and his neighbours (who Kirk was yet to meet). With his earlier contented mood rapidly waning, Kirk pushed his plate away, swallowed his beer and bade the publican goodnight, relieved at last to reach his room.

He pushed the door open to the veranda and leaned on the balustrade. A full moon beamed silver light on the street, highlighting a fox trotting boldly across the road while, from a tree nearby, a Boobook owl hooted.

A sense of peace enveloped him and he clasped his hands together, breathing in the chilly night air. Winter was here, and, although nothing like the icy, bone-aching cold of the Snowy Mountains, it was bracing, demonstrating a clean freshness that Kirk welcomed.

He mulled over Neil's offer—a list of projects including preparing new garden beds for spring, freshening the old home with a coat of paint, and building an animal nursery that would entice families to come and stay. The three months Kirk had planned to be away stretched into eternity and his thoughts returned to his house in Dalgety. Should he contact a real estate agent and have it rented out for the rest of the year? Perhaps by then, he would have had enough time to explore the area, delve into the mystery surrounding the non-existent Turtle Ridge—and get to know a certain attractive landowner a little better.

Returning to his bedroom, the stuffiness hit him and he groaned. Staying here with his feet hanging over the end of the double bed and eating Ned's cooking was one step too far.

I need to find somewhere else to stay.

THE DOORBELL PINGED as Kirk entered the store, surprised to see Frank at the counter.

'G'day mate. Day off today?' the older man asked.

'Yeah. Valerie's supposed to be home this weekend so it's time for a breather for us all.' Kirk returned Frank's smile and drew a deep breath. 'Don't suppose you know of anywhere I could rent for a few months?'

Frank chuckled, his balding head shaking. 'Wondered how long you'd put up with old Ned. I hear his food's edible, but not exactly appetising.' He rubbed his unshaven chin and met Kirk's eyes.

'His meals are appreciated—don't misunderstand me. It's just ... I'm used to living alone, and it looks like I'll be around for a while, so thought I might as well get comfortable.'

'W-ell.' Frank drawled. 'There's not much about in a town this size, but I could ask Lola if she knows what's happening with old Mrs Coonan's place. She died a while back see—and as far as I know, the family are still squabbling over who gets what. Seems it'll be a few months yet before they sort it out.'

'Where is this place?'

'On the road up to Featherwood Station. Easy to miss. It's an old cottage tucked amongst a heap of trees.'

'Would you have a contact number for the family?'

Frank scrabbled about in a drawer under the counter before throwing his hands up in defeat. 'I'll have to ask Lola. Hang on a tick. She's pegging out the washing.'

Kirk nodded, and while Frank disappeared out the back, he browsed the newspaper headlines on the stand. A frisson of hope heightened his mood and he raised his eyebrows hopefully when Frank returned.

'Knew she'd have it stashed somewhere.' He opened the till and withdrew a neatly folded envelope from its recesses before handing it to Kirk.

Pulling his phone from his pocket, Kirk loaded the information onto it and handed the envelope back. 'Thanks, Frank. I'll give them a ring.'

'Goodo. Let us know how you get on.'

Kirk flicked a hand in response and walked up the hill to where a neatly maintained park housed a table and benches, flanked by a barbeque for use by passing travellers.

Half an hour later, he revisited the store, a smile spreading across his face.

'How'd you get on?' Lola put her knitting down and rose from her chair. There was no sign of Frank.

'Okay, thanks. The lady I spoke to had to ring her siblings for approval to rent the cottage out and will be phoning you for a reference if you don't mind?'

'Oh.' Lola wrinkled her brow. 'I'll have to be honest and say I don't really know you—but I'm happy to give them any information I can. Will that do?'

'Thanks Lola. Hopefully that's all they'll need. She said I can stay there for three months and they'll review it after that.'

'I heard Neil's pretty happy with your work.' She grinned and tucked a loose strand of grey hair behind her ear. 'Sounds like you might get a bit more employment—if you want it?'

Kirk ducked his head. 'Yeah. I guess we'll see what the next couple of months bring. I'd still like to go bush and explore the area my grandfather spoke of.'

Lola sniffed. 'Well, you'd better speak to Ginny about that—and wait until winter's over.'

'I see.' He hid his surprise and continued. 'Why Ginny?'

Lola's jaw dropped. "Don't you know?'

Kirk shook his head. 'Know what?'

'Featherwood Station owns the land that leads right up into the hills—to where the old mines used to be. If you want to explore anything up that way, you'll need to get her permission. Not only that.' She paused, emitting a gentle snort. 'You've picked the wrong time of the year. I gets pretty cold up there. Better off waiting until spring.

'Right. Thanks for the heads up.'

Placing his meagre groceries on the counter, he fished his wallet out of his pocket with a faint grin hovering around his mouth. *The coldest place in Queensland would be no match for the Snowy Mountains—and he was used to it.*

He was almost at the door when Lola asked, 'I guess the cottage is still furnished?'

'Apparently, yes. They said there's even some old linen and kitchen utensils I can use, but the personal stuff has been removed.' He lifted a hand in acknowledgement. 'Thanks again for your help—and Frank's. Much obliged.'

A soft smile crept over his face as he walked to the pub, dwelling on Lola's friendly face. *It seems some townsfolk have accepted I'm here to stay ...for a while. Things are looking up.*

15

'Hi Lola.' Ginny grinned at her friend, shutting the door behind her.

'Hello love. I was only thinking of you this morning. Haven't seen you for a couple of weeks. Everything okay?'

Ginny sighed. 'Yeah. Been busy though. The frosts the last few mornings have made a hole in my woodpile so I've been trying to chop more—not very well, I'm afraid.'

'Oh, you need "The Man from Snowy River". I'm sure he won't take long to cut you enough to last all winter.' She chortled and Ginny's cheeks flushed pink.

'Very funny.'

'Cuppa?' Lola turned toward the kitchen without waiting for Ginny's reply.

'Thanks. I've lost track of the weeks but I think it's

my turn to give a hand with the tuckshop orders next week. Is that right?' She followed Lola into the kitchen.

'I've been thinking. You've helped for years and there's a few mothers who want to give a hand now. Why don't you concentrate on your farm and leave me to worry about the school? You're welcome to pop in for a cuppa any time that suits, without having to think about what day it is.'

A wave of relief washed over Ginny and she smiled. 'That sounds great. Don't let on to Donald, but some days I struggle.'

Lola narrowed her eyes. 'What does Donald have to do with it? I don't see much of him anyway—although young Andrew popped in the other day.'

'Yeah. He gave me a hand with some cattle—and was keen to show off his new ute.'

Lola grunted. 'Of course. So carry on. What's Donald been up to?'

'Nothing really. Just ensuring I know he would be more than happy to take over Featherwood Station and let me settle into a "nice little house in town" as he puts it.'

Lola frowned, tut-tutting. 'That man! I could never understand how two brothers could be so different. I hope you put him in his place.'

'I certainly did—but I can't help but wonder if that's the real reason for Andrew turning up. He's a nice boy but his gentle nature stops him from standing up to his father. Shame he doesn't have siblings. They may have helped?'

'Or not! He's a prime candidate for his father's bullying.' Lola poured the tea and removed the lid from a cake tin. 'Fruit cake?'

Ginny shrugged. 'Why not. It's weird. I've struggled with weight gain for years and now my clothes are getting loose on me. The result of not having a family to feed, I suppose." She dived a hand into the tin and grinned. 'Your cakes are always so much nicer than mine too.'

Concern filled Lola's eyes. 'Don't you go getting all skinny now. You're doing hard work and need your strength.' She pushed the tin closer to Ginny. 'Eat up while I fetch something I want to show you.'

A soft, secretive smile spread over Lola's face as she left the room. Seconds later she returned with a small bundle wrapped in an old, knitted jumper. She lowered it onto Ginny's lap and carefully prised the top open.

'Aww. Isn't it gorgeous?' Ginny smiled as two huge eyes peered up at her. 'A baby possum?'

'Yes. Frank found it a few days ago while he was doing the mail run. It's mother had been killed by a car and it was still clinging to her back—poor little tike.'

Ginny stroked the velvety head. 'It's lucky to have survived.'

'Yes. I didn't think she'd make it the first night, but she's pretty determined it seems.'

'Another one for your menagerie out the back then?' Ginny chuckled and Lola rolled her eyes.

'That's what Frank said. He's a good man though—said he'd add another section to the row of "hospital cages" and we'll put her out with that little Brush-Tail I reared during the summer. Then they'll have company until they're old enough to go into the big aviary.'

Ginny nodded. Frank and Lola's love of wildlife had increased over the years and now their small acreage was smothered with as many respite facilities as they could fit in. Ginny didn't know how they managed it but assumed it had grown from a need after their only son left home, to a habit they didn't want to relinquish. During drought years, Frank created feed and water dishes in the bush behind their property so the wildlife could find water and not starve.

Lola rose and removed the baby possum from Ginny. 'I'd better get this little one out of the kitchen,' she whispered. 'Last thing we need if a health officer walked into the shop for a random check.'

'Oh, of course.' Ginny gave a small shake of her head as Lola left the room. Used to allowing her own pets inside, she'd forgotten how strict the health rules were for businesses.

She stood and rinsed their cups under the tap.

'So what's next on your agenda.'

Ginny whipped around at Lola's words.

'Oh! I didn't hear you come in. Must have been miles away.' Ginny shrugged. 'I guess I'll organise Kirk to chop wood for me—and while he's here, he can check the shed again. I know I'm being a bit paranoid about those termites, but the woolshed is such an important building. I couldn't manage without it.'

Lola patted her arm. 'I'm sure all is well now and you're worrying over nothing.' She sighed sympathetically. 'It's been a tough year for you—but you're keeping your head above water so that's the main thing and you can have a bit of a rest over winter, can't you?'

'Not exactly. I know there's no sheep work to be done for a couple of months, but I still need to check the stock every few days—and now winter's here I'll have to start feeding out hay.'

'Speaking of hay, did you hear Nigel's bought Terry Collins hay-making machinery. Terry's had enough and apparently Nigel wants to expand his income opportunities. Lord knows why. He's got all those vegetables, fruit trees and his cattle. Isn't that enough for one man?'

Ginny stared at her. 'No. I hadn't heard that.' She frowned.

'What are you thinking?' Lola asked.

'Nigel came to see me on the anniversary of Lyndon's death. I must have forgotten to tell you.

Anyway, he offered to help me at first. Then he said if I decided I couldn't cope, he'd like to buy Featherwood Station.'

'What!' Lola choked. 'He has enough trouble keeping staff—how does he think he'd cope with more land?' She paused and huffed out a noisy breath. 'I reckon that man has delusions of being king of Featherwood Falls. Huh! I hope you sent him packing?'

Ginny smiled. 'I politely declined his offer but said I'd call if I needed him.'

Lola burst into laughter as the front door bell pinged. She gave Ginny a brief hug. 'I'd better see who this is. Will you stay for lunch?'

Ginny shook her head as they walked into the shop. 'Thanks, but no. I've got things to do at home. I'll call in again soon.'

As she left the store she smiled at the woman browsing the ice-cream freezer before observing the smart four wheel drive vehicle and pristine caravan parked on the roadside.

'Enjoy your holiday,' Ginny said.

The woman looked up and returned her smile. 'Thanks.'

Hmm, Featherwood Falls is getting popular.

IT HAD BEEN two weeks since the vet had visited, and, thinking over what she'd said to Lola, Ginny decided she'd spend the afternoon doing the rounds of the stock.

Her heart leapt. Kirk's vehicle was parked in the yard—and yet the dogs were quiet? She smiled. It hadn't taken them long to realise he was no threat. Before she had time to get out of the car, his tall, denim-clad figure filled her rear-vision mirror. She grabbed her bag and stepped out to greet him.

'Hi stranger.'

He shuffled his feet. 'Hi. Sorry. I've been a bit slack. Meant to get back before now.'

'That's okay. Are you here to give the shed another spray?'

'Yes. I had more work at Kallala than I had expected. Have to go back again too.'

'Kallala?'

'That's what Neil and Valerie have called the place. Looks like I'll be there all winter.'

'Oh?'

'They've got grand plans of setting it up as a holiday farm—with a petting zoo and all that stuff. Also planning to convert that old packing shed into some sort of barn for weddings and other events.'

'Wow! Good on them.' She pushed the gate open. 'Would you like a cuppa before you start?'

'Thanks. Wouldn't say no.'

Minutes later, they were sitting opposite each other at the dining table with the fire roaring at the end of the room.

'Umm. I was wondering if you would have time to cut some wood for me—if you're not too busy on Kallala that is?'

'Sure. I'm moving out of the pub over the weekend and will be living close by, so any time you need a hand, let me know.'

Ginny leaned forward, clasping her hands around her mug. 'Really? Where?'

'I'm renting Mrs Coonan's place for the winter while her family sort out what they're going to do with it. Hopefully by then the weather will be warm enough for me to head for the hills.' He grinned. 'Depending on you, of course.'

'Why me?'

'Lola mentioned you own the land that leads to where my grandfather spoke about. Turtle Ridge, or the Camel Hump. It's where he found a rock that indicated tin ore and hoped to return to fulfil a hankering for a bit of prospecting one day. He died before he could get to it ... so I thought I'd like to take a look for myself.'

'I see. Well, I have no problem with you going through my land—but you should know no-one has been up there for decades. Some of the old timers around here reckon the old mine sites are haunted. A few attempts have been made to grow dope on the land behind the mines, but the last few years have been so dry I reckon they would have struggled, even if they hadn't been caught.'

She inclined her head while he absorbed the information. Hesitantly, she continued. 'I've got a couple of jobs to do around here, then I'm going to check both the cattle and sheep. If you've got nothing else to do, you might like to join me? I could show you the old track the miner's used to use. It's mostly covered over now but follows the creek right up into the hills.'

'Sounds great. I've got the spray mixed up for the shed so it's only a matter of putting my protective gear on and getting onto it. Probably take about half an hour.'

'Okay. It's a deal. Did you know you'll have to walk the last few kilometres if you want to reach the mine site?'

He rubbed a work-roughened hand over his beard as a slow grin spread over his face. 'I assumed I would. Got all the gear so there's no worries there.'

Ginny gave a small nod as Kirk pushed his chair back and rose to his feet. 'Thanks for the cuppa. When we get back, I'll chop a load of wood for you and come back tomorrow to do the rest if you like?'

'Thanks. Sounds great—but didn't you say you're moving in to Mrs Coonan's?'

He laughed, a deep, hearty sound that oozed

strength. 'I reckon that'll take me all of half an hour. The house is still furnished apparently—even has linen and kitchen stuff.'

'Good.' She wrinkled her nose. 'You might have to pick up a few mouse traps and cleaning stuff from Lola. It's been empty for a while now and I don't think anyone has been here to check it for months.'

'I'm sure it won't take long.' He pulled his boots on and headed outside, leaving Ginny staring after him.

With renewed vigour, she raced out to the clothesline, pulled the sheets off and briskly folded and stowed them in the linen cupboard. Then she chopped up meat and vegetables and filled the slow cooker before nipping to the bathroom. Regretting she hadn't washed her hair that morning, she brushed it, clipping the sides back with combs and allowing the wavy locks to rest on her shoulders. Swiping lip gloss over her mouth, she smiled at the bright hazel eyes in the mirror and headed back to the living room where she stoked the fire, waited for it to catch, and then closed the flue.

'Right. Everything's sorted.' She grinned at the three cats lounging on the hearth rug. 'I'll leave you lot in charge.'

Locking the door behind her, she bounced down the steps, the keys to the Toyota in her hand.

16

*G*inny rested her elbow on the open window and, with the fresh winter breeze filling the cab, she breathed deeply. The man sitting beside her filled the ute with more than just his solid presence. His huge hands rested lightly in his lap and a feeling of calm excitement wafted over her, despite the restlessness of the dogs on the back tray of the ute.

'Great views over the valley.' Kirk's comment broke the silence and Ginny smiled.

'I know. I love it. It gives me a sense of freedom.' She chuckled. 'I'm a bit of a sook when it comes to small places and confinement.'

'Huh. I sympathise. A bit claustrophobic myself. Guess that's why I prefer outdoor work.'

She pulled up at the gate and Kirk leapt out to

open it. The dogs leaned toward the edge of the tray in anticipation.

'Stay!' Ginny ordered and all five dropped to their bellies again.

She drove through the opening, casting her gaze around the paddock of ewes and lambs while she waited. Everything appeared normal, the lambs now big enough to graze alongside their mothers.

'They look great, don't they?' Kirk slid back into his seat, shooting Ginny a respectful glance.

She smiled and changed gear. 'Yes. I usually start giving them extra feed from about the end of July. For the moment though, there's still plenty of grass.'

They bumped across the track for the next half hour, pausing to open and shut gates and check water troughs. Reaching a crest facing west, Ginny halted on the ridge overlooking the farthest portion of Feather-wood's land. In front of them, black Angus cattle grazed, spread across the vast pasture.

Ginny narrowed her eyes. Indicating the glove compartment in front of Kirk, she said, 'Would you mind getting the binoculars out for me please?'

He passed them to her with a questioning angle to his head. 'Is everything alright?'

'Not sure. There seem too many cattle here. There should be a hundred and twenty four. The remaining sixteen that weren't in calf went back to the bulls. They should be on the other side of those trees, closer to the yards.' She pointed to a row of dark pines in the distance before holding the binoculars to her eyes. Handing them to Kirk, she continued. 'I hope I've made a mistake, but to me, it looks very much like the bulls sitting under those trees, on this side of the fence.'

She waited while Kirk scanned the paddock through the binoculars.

He lowered them to his lap and faced her. Her stomach sank at the grim look on his face.

'You're right. Those two at the bottom of the paddock are definitely bulls, and at a quick glance, I'd say you've got more than you thought you did.'

'I don't understand. Andrew spent all afternoon helping us preg-test them all and he waited until I'd brought the pregnant ones here before he shifted the rest.'

'So ... were they in adjacent paddocks?'

'No!' She didn't mean to speak sharply. Kirk appeared not to have noticed.

'Let's take a closer look.' He spoke calmly and Ginny drew a deep breath and nodded.

'There were two paddocks between them—and I checked that all gates were closed before I left.' Her voice caught with frustration. 'I know bulls can be rough on fences which is why I thought it best to put the dry cows with them. You know, keep them occupied.' She grunted. 'Occupied is right,' she muttered. 'They better not have smashed all the fences to bits.'

Concern knotted in her stomach as they approached the bottom fence line. The fence appeared intact, however the adjoining gate was flung wide and had caught on a small rock, lodging it firmly open. Ginny frowned and let her gaze roam across the field to where the bulls and sixteen dry cows should have been. She squinted, slamming the ute into gear.

'I don't believe it. All the gates are open!'

The ute roared over the grass, dodging rocks as they travelled and Kirk grabbed the dash. 'You're sure Andrew understood your instructions?'

'Of course. He's lived on a farm all his life and knows the golden rule of ensuring all gates are closed —unless of course, they've been opened for a purpose. And this was definitely not one of those occasions.'

Kirk didn't reply, instead waiting for Ginny to stop and turn the engine off. He stepped out and strode to the gate, inspecting the latch.

Ginny leaned on the strainer post, fingering the chain that hung from its solid, steel U-bolt.

'I see you use a double chain with both a hook and a carabiner. No chance of the cattle working that one out.' He rubbed a hand over his face and squatted in the dirt. 'No tracks either, or signs of the post being rubbed by a bull, potentially undoing the chain.'

'Lyndon was extremely particular with his cattle

and over the years, did everything he could to ensure the security of our stock.' Ginny's voice quavered.

Kirk's hand rested on her arm, it's warmth sending a shock wave through her. She choked back the lump in her throat, and straightened her shoulders, determined not to weaken.

'I hate to admit it Ginny, but I suspect someone has tampered with these gates.' Kirk's voice was low and serious.

Ginny clung to the fence post as the strength drained from her legs. *Lyndon, the potential fire, windmill issue and now this? Why?*

'Are you okay?' Kirk gripped Ginny's elbow, his strength flowing into her.

'Y-yes. At least I think so.' Suddenly Lola's comment from weeks ago about not trusting strangers flared in her memory and she stared at Kirk. Could he have been responsible for these incidents? Surely not.

Her confidence wavered as her gaze met his. 'I suppose I'd better report it to Stan.'

'The cop?'

'Yes. He came out and had a look at the windmill when I found someone had turned it off and the cattle were thirsty.'

'And?'

She shook her head. 'He didn't think I had evidence to prove it wasn't my own doing—suggested I may have forgotten. Even the fire—he dismissed that as either you or I leaving the drum there and it being knocked over by a dog or fox.'

Kirk frowned, his lips a thin line in the forest of black beard. 'I didn't use kerosene. I told you. I burned the rotten wood but it was out in the middle of the track and all I had to do was drop a match and it was ashes within minutes. Other than that, I used my little generator for the repairs and made sure it was full and ready for use before I left the pub.'

His voice was quiet, his concentration appearing to drift.

'So, what do you think I should do?' Ginny asked. Guilt stabbed at her. How could she possibly think he had anything to do with it? The man had been so helpful.

Kirk blinked at her, as though suddenly remembering she was there. 'I guess we'd better get the cattle back to the yards, draft them into their respective herds. It might be a good idea to check them more regularly to ensure this doesn't happen again.'

Ginny sighed. It was already mid-afternoon and it would be dark by five thirty.

'You're right.' She released the dogs from their chains and sent them around the herd. Within seconds the team of kelpies had gathered them together in a sea of black.

An hour later, Ginny let out a relieved breath and shot Kirk a smile.

'I thought we might have had more trouble than that. Thank goodness I put a dot of paint on those not in calf—even if it had faded.'

He grinned. 'Sure was. I reckon you might have had to get the vet back if you hadn't.'

'I probably would have just let it go—even if it wasn't good practice.' Pointing to the sinking sun, she added, 'Won't be long before we're in darkness here. I'll take the cows in calf back to where they were and leave the rest here until morning.'

'Righto. I'll give you a hand.'

THE SUN WAS SINKING QUICKLY, the temperature plummeting. Ginny turned the heater up to full and a thin trickle of warm air did its best to increase the temperature in the drafty vehicle.

'Burr! There's a nip in the air.' Kirk rubbed his arms as he slid into the passenger seat. 'Lucky I'm used to it.'

Ginny grinned at him. 'Thanks for your help today.'

'My pleasure.' His voice was low, with a timbre that warmed Ginny's soul.

She accelerated up the rise, slowing when they reached the top and turned onto the track that led back to the homestead.

'It'll be dark shortly. Would you like to stay for

dinner? I've got the slow cooker on and dinner should be ready by the time we get back. Nothing fancy.'

'Thanks. If it's not too much trouble, I'd like that.'

Her pulse pounded in her chest. *What am I saying?*

In the still, cold night air, their conversation halted while the ute rattled over the bumps, eventually resting beside the dog kennels.

'I hope you don't mind waiting while I feed the dogs?'

Kirk shook his head and laughed. 'Of course not. I'm sure I can do something to help. Would you like me to take hay back to the cattle in the yards while you sort things out here?'

Gratitude filled Ginny. Used to performing the routine tasks alone, Kirk's offer came as a surprise.

'Um. That would be wonderful. Thanks.' She pointed to the hay shed tucked against the pine trees in the lea of the hill. 'There's some in the shed. Three or four bales should be plenty for the night. I'll move them tomorrow—to somewhere closer so I can keep an eye on them.'

'Righto. I won't be long and when I get back, I'll split a heap of that wood for you while you're organising dinner.' He inclined his head to the pile of humungous lumps of wood resting against the fence that ran along the back of the house. A small wood-shed backed against a gnarly Pepperina tree with a massive chopping block beside it, the head of an axe buried in its grey and weathered surface.

While Kirk slid behind the steering wheel of the ute, Ginny fed and locked up the dogs, filled water containers and checked on the chooks.

Minutes later, she heard the vehicle accelerate away while she hurried to the house. Cold and dark, she switched on all the lights and stoked the fire before stirring the contents of the slow cooker.

Oscar stalked across the floor, his tail held aloft and emitting a demanding meow.

'You want your dinner first I suppose.' Ginny bent and picked up the cat, moved to the pantry and scooped a cupful of cat kibble from the container. Then, opening the door onto the veranda, she tipped the food into the bowl and lowered Oscar to the floor. 'That will have to keep you going while I finish getting dinner.'

She glanced at her watch and strode to the bathroom.

If I'm quick, I'll have time. She stripped off and stepped into the shower. Minutes later, hair brushed and hanging loose around her face, she pulled on clean jeans and a warm jumper, and returned to the kitchen.

The casserole was bubbling fragrantly when the familiar sound of the farm ute approached. A door slammed and Ginny's heart surged.

It had been a long time since she had entertained anyone for dinner—and she dithered. *Am I doing the right thing? What if he thinks I'm interested in him?* She shook her head as his footsteps crossed the veranda. *Of course not. I'm being hospitable and neighbourly. That's all.*

17

*H*eat rose up Ginny's face as Kirk, laden with an armload of firewood entered the room.

'Smells good.' He grinned and dropped the wood in the box next to the fire. Then he brushed off his hands. 'Do you mind if I clean up?'

'Of course. Follow me.'

They crossed the polished timber floor and walked down the hallway. Ginny stepped aside, waving an arm toward the large, farmhouse bathroom. A roll-top bath sat along the wall beneath a leadlight window with a separate shower filling the corner. Occupying the space between the doorway to the shower was a long vanity unit with a marble bench top, and in the opposite corner, an old-fashioned toilet sat, its raised cistern fastened to the wall with a porcelain handled chain hanging from it.

'Wow. What a lovely bathroom.' Kirk glanced around the room before meeting Ginny's eyes with an admiring smile.

'It's very old but we gave it a face lift a few years ago —more of an antique maintenance project than a renovation, except for the new shower.'

She pointed to a folded green towel on the edge of the bath. 'I'll leave you to it and finish preparing dinner.'

He nodded and she turned away and trod quietly to the kitchen.

An hour later, satisfied by the hearty meal and warmed by the heat from the blazing fire, Ginny placed a mug of tea each on the coffee table and turned hesitantly to Kirk.

'Would you like to watch a movie?'

'Sure. It's been a while since I saw anything on TV. In the pub it was Ned's company and sport ... and, without sounding rude, neither appealed much.'

Ginny bent her head back and laughed. 'I can understand that. Poor Ned. He means well but he hasn't been the same since his wife died. The pub's been his life I suppose—and he's not one for change.'

She plonked herself on the couch and picked up the remote. He lowered himself beside her, shoved a cushion behind his back and stretched out his long legs.

'What do you like to watch?' She flicked onto Netflix and scrolled through a range of movies. 'Thrillers, drama, war movies. Any favourites?'

In the end, they settled on a movie that neither had seen, but had both read the book many years earlier—*Captain Corelli's Mandolin.*

As the movie progressed, Ginny unwound slowly, the clean fresh scent of soap mixed with the maleness of her companion heightening her senses. It was almost eleven before the film finished and they glanced at each other, sharing a soft smile.

'That was beautiful. Thank you.' Kirk reached out his hand and grasped hers.

She squeezed his back and smiled as her stomach leaped. 'Thanks for seeing it through.'

He pushed himself to his feet and stretched. 'I'd better leave you to sleep now. It's late and we've got plenty to keep us busy tomorrow.'

She smiled, forcing herself to breathe evenly to quell her rising elation. 'Thanks again for your help today. Are you back at Kallala in the morning?'

'Yes. I'll be working five days a week for Neil—over winter anyway. But, if there's anything you'd like a hand with, let me know. There's still two days a week to fill.' He shot her a small grin.

'I'll remember that. Thank you.'

At the veranda door, he pulled his boots on, stepped closer to her, and paused. 'Don't come outside. It's freezing.' He leaned forward and gave her a peck on the cheek, turned and disappeared into the dark.

Ginny touched the spot he had kissed, her eyes widening as the sound of his LandCruiser rumbled into the distance. Glancing up at the family photo, her lip quivered.

'I'm sorry Lyndon. I don't know what to do.'

WEARINESS SLOWED GINNY'S MOVEMENTS—AND her thinking–the following morning. The process of moving the small herd of cattle from the yards to a fresh paddock took hours as Ginny's mind replayed the events of the previous evening. She allowed guilt to vie with justification, draining the last of her energy. At last, with the cattle settled and animals fed, she returned with relief to the couch in the lounge and stretched out, her head on the cushion that, only a few hours ago, had been at Kirk's back.

The phone rang and she struggled upright, shuffled to the kitchen, and answered it.

'Hello?'

'Hi Mum. It's me.'

Ginny smiled at the sound of Briony's voice.

'Hi love. How are things?'

'Great!' Ginny raised her eyebrows at her daughter's enthusiasm. This was a change from the morose young woman who had phoned only a week ago.

'What's happened? You sound very happy.'

'I am. Scotland's lifted more restrictions and we've been getting so many bookings, it looks as though I'll have plenty of work until the end of the season.'

'Phew. That is good news.' Only days before, Briony had been so down in the dumps that Ginny had been worried about her state of mind. The remote hotel she worked in had all but closed and staff that remained were unable to receive a wage until they reopened. Ginny had consoled her by pointing out that at least she had free board and food, which was more than many others around the world.

It hadn't helped at the time and Briony had finished the call and hung up. Now Ginny listened to her excited daughter as she retreated to the couch again, allowing her shoulders to relax. *One less worry.*

'Are you still planning to come home for Christmas?'

'Absolutely. I'm hoping Alex will change his mind and come too—but we'll see. He's a bit nervous about travelling at the moment.'

'I understand. It will be good to have you girls home though.'

'You sound tired Mum. Are you okay?'

'Oh yes. I'm fine. I had a late night last night, that's all. Watched a movie.'

'Great. On your own?'

Ginny hesitated. Until now, she had not mentioned Kirk to her daughters, except to tell them she had found a handyman to fix the woolshed.

'No. Actually, the man I mentioned was giving me a hand with maintenance called in yesterday and helped me with some cattle work so I asked him to stay for tea.' She held her breath, expecting a disapproving retort from Briony.

'Good on you.'

Ginny lifted her chin in astonishment.

'You approve?'

'Of course I do. Mum, it's been well over a year since Dad died and he wouldn't want you to slog your guts out on the farm without some sort of social life.'

Ginny wasn't so sure. 'Do you really think so?'

Briony snorted down the phone. 'Of course I do. You're only forty-eight so not exactly over the hill. If you meet someone nice, and trustworthy, I say go for it.'

Nice—yes. Trustworthy—Ginny faltered. She had not seen anything to doubt his trust, no matter what others said.

'Thanks, love. I appreciate your trust too. We're only friends though. I'm not interested—or ready for anything more.'

'Well, whatever way it goes, I know you'll do the right thing and I also know Dad would not be wanting you to live the rest of your life like a bitter old maid.'

'Huh!' Ginny retorted. Was she heading down that path? Of course not. She only wanted to seek the truth about Lyndon's death.

'I'd better go now Mum. Talk again next week.'

'Okay, bye love. Have a good week.'

'I will. Bye.'

Ginny hit the red button and lay the handpiece on the coffee table. Her heart lightened and she allowed a small smile to creep onto her face.

Glancing at the cats curled on the hearthrug, she rose to her feet and looked out the window. The winter sun shone, its rays filtering through the glass. The trees were still and a magpie sat on the veranda railing, warbling a tuneful song. Ginny nodded to herself.

'Yep. A perfect day for a ride.'

REASSURED BY BRIONY'S COMMENTS, Ginny urged Akela into a brisk trot, the smile spreading across her face. With the five dogs running beside them, taking care to keep their distance from the mare, Ginny gulped the fresh clean air and cast her gaze over the ground. Her smile waned as frost damage became more evident— the honey coloured grass, crisp and dry. Here and there, small patches of clover appeared amongst the foliage.

'At least that should keep the boys going,' she muttered, crossing her fingers.

In a few weeks' time, the shearers would be turning up to shear the merino wethers and Ginny did a mental calculation as the fug cleared from her head. *What should take precedence now?*

Her mind churned, ticking off the routine steps in Lyndon's annual plan. Methodical and reliable, every year of their marriage he had followed the same pattern with little variation. Ginny pursed her lips, cringing in the saddle. He would have sorted out the young cattle by now, selling the marketable stock to protect the winter feed for spring calves and lambs. Then, as temperatures warmed, shearing would begin and a month later, calves would arrive as spring coloured the valley. By late September, the stud ewes that hadn't given birth in autumn, would begin producing their lambs—and somewhere amongst that, the field of lucerne would need mowing and baling. Ginny sighed before urging Akela into a canter. By the time the shed was filled with sweet-smelling hay, Briony and Claire would be making their Christmas plans—and summer would be here for them to enjoy life together.

The rhythmic pounding of the horse's hooves

matched the thud of her heart and as she rode, Ginny's mood lifted.

I can do this Lyndon. I might not have taken as much notice as I should have, but this is my farm now—and I will make it better than it's ever been.

She grasped the reins in her left hand and waved her right in the air, whooping.

'Look out whoever's trying to frighten me! It's not happening!'

18

Kirk was late. Still adjusting to the musty smell of the old cottage and the scrabbling of rats and mice in the roof, his night had been short. For the first time in years, he slept passed day break, waking with a start as the morning sun filtered through the overgrown trees and flickered across the quilt.

Confused, his waking dream faded into scrambled, disturbing shards. Two women, one younger than the other, both hazel eyed and pleading. As the younger one disappeared into blackness, it was Ginny who stood there, smiling at him. He cursed. 'It's Katie I should be thinking about, not a random landowner that I happen to have given a helping hand', he muttered. He dressed hastily and splashed cold water over his face before heading for the kitchen.

Glancing at the faded picture of the Queen on the wall, he swallowed the last mouthful of toast, emptied the coffee mug, and dropped three apples and a large water bottle into his esky. Grabbing the keys, he closed the door tightly behind him and drove to the store.

'Morning Lola.'

She frowned. 'You're a bit late this morning. No work?'

He sighed and responded firmly. 'Yes—at Kallala. I'm running late. Could I have a couple of your meat and vegetable pasties please?'

She shot a sideways glance at him, her eyebrows raised at his brisk tone as she reached into the warmer.

'Anything wrong?'

He shook his head. 'No. I apologise. Too many vermin in the ceiling disturbing my sleep, that's all.'

'Oh, I see.' She chuckled. 'If you like, I'll send Frank up there this afternoon to put a few traps and baits around the place. Perhaps you need a cat?'

He returned her smile and shrugged. 'Thanks. A cat might work—until I move on. Then what would I do?'

She rubbed her palms over her cheeks as she studied him. 'Ahh. I reckon you'll be around a bit longer than you think. Nigel's the only one around here who's workers flit away quickly. Stay away from his place and you never know what might happen,' she finished with a cheeky grin.

'Thanks.' He turned quickly and left the store, thankful his beard hid the deepening colour on his face.

Driving away, he changed gears fiercely, blustering to himself. 'Bloody small town gossip. How the hell does she know what I'm thinking—or where I go?' But deep within, a spark smouldered and a smile crept across his face.

GRATEFUL FOR THE company of Neil and the increasing amount of work required, Kirk settled into the house painting with gusto, leaving Neil to work on the door and window frames while he focused on the eaves and guttering. They hoped to finish the fiddly bits this week and get on to the walls while the weather was sunny and dry.

While the previous pleasant evening continued to warm his heart, a sliver of panic crept in. He wasn't ready for anything more than friendship and the last thing he needed was a tie.

Mulling over his life as the brush swept rhythmically back and forth, his mind drifted back to the fourteen years of marriage to Katie. At first it had been wonderful, their joint enthusiasm for the mountains including skiing in the winter and hiking during the summer—the glue that kept them united. When Katie had announced she was pregnant after eight years of trying, their love blossomed further and Kirk counted the days until their child joined them, forming a 'real' family.

But then things had gone wrong. Their stillborn daughter had triggered a long, depressive period for Katie. She refused to try again, moved herself to the spare bedroom and retreated into a bitter, silent shell.

Helpless and consumed with his own sadness, Kirk looked back now, knowing he should have done more. He hadn't known where to start—and both of them hid the depths of their trouble from family members rather than face it.

Then, almost two years after their baby's funeral, and unbeknown to him, Katie found a lump in her breast. Insignificant and painless, she had ignored it until one day, when Kirk entered the bathroom as she was dressing, he noticed the puckered skin and irregular shape of one of her once perfect breasts.

Shocked, he had forced her to see a doctor and accompanied her to every appointment that followed. In a silent daze, she had agreed and surgery, chemotherapy, radiation, and constant sickness had followed.

Under Kirk's care, their love rekindled—to a degree. Although they knew it was too late, the periods of remission that followed allowed them to return to a semblance of normality. Katie moved back into the main bedroom and they even managed a few enjoyable days of skiing.

Then, the cancer returned with a vengeance—and Kirk's life once again became a merry-go-round. While continuing to work when he could, others took turns to care for Katie, clean their house and prepare a never ending supply of meals which only he could eat. The palliative care team took over and Katie was moved to a Hospice in Cooma.

'Coming in for a cuppa, Kirk?'

Kirk glanced up, startled at Neil's call.

'Sure. Thanks. I'll be right up.'

Dismissing his period of reminiscence, he plastered a smile on his face, wrapped his paint brush in plastic wrap to prevent it from drying out, and followed Neil inside.

A fire burned brightly and the air was filled with the smell of fresh scones. Kirk tilted his head back and sniffed, grinning at Valerie.

'Something smells good.'

She chuckled. 'I thought you fella's would be looking for something nice after all those weeks of faring for yourselves.'

Neil wrapped his arm around her shoulders. 'It's good to have you home again—and not just for your cooking.' He winked and she flicked the tea-towel at him.

'Go on, sit down and get stuck in while they're hot.'

Kirk pulled out the chair and shot her a smile, a little surprised at the similarity in looks between husband and wife. Although well in their fifties, both were vibrant, active, and fair-haired with not a grey strand to be seen. Tall and lean, Neil had a long, pleasant face that wore a permanently happy expression while Valerie's slight, energetic build was smaller, reminding Kirk of the wrens that flittered constantly in and out of the shrubs.

Was that what attracted him to Ginny? The gentle smile that rarely left her face, despite her workload and the sadness that she had endured.

'Help yourself, Kirk.'

His attention darted back to the bright, friendly woman sitting opposite him as she passed the plate of scones.

Taking one, he smiled as she held a bowl of whipped cream in the other hand. Steam wafted upward as he split it open and Neil slid a dish of jam toward him.

Memories of childhood flittered—his grandmother's scones, the huge table in the Cooma dining room, and his grandfather's whispered words.

'One day I'm going back there and I'll be a rich man.'

Here he was, in the small town his grandfather had referred to—knowing it would be months before he had a hope of beginning his search, and absolutely no idea what the old man had been talking about.

19

*A*s winter progressed, Ginny filled her days weeding the overgrown vegetable patch, feeding hay, catching up with her mother, and checking her stock. After the baffling events of the previous weeks, Ginny's confidence had taken a hit. She'd had to tighten the belt on her jeans another notch and dark rings shadowed her eyes. Taking the dogs everywhere with her became habit, even when their assistance was not needed, their company reassuring her she was not alone, despite their lack of ability to speak. When all appeared to have returned to normal after a month, she relaxed, convincing herself perhaps the kerosene tin had been at the shed and she hadn't noticed. The windmill was still a puzzle but again, she persuaded herself that perhaps Stan was right—maybe she had tied it off to grease the gears and had forgotten to release it again?

Her afternoon routine of bringing firewood inside triggered thoughts of Kirk, despite the recent lack of contact with him. A smile softened her face as she recollected the note he had put on her door. Most people would have simply turned up when it suited them, but his written apology for not spraying the shed as promised, showed consideration. She revelled in the knowledge, and thoughts of new beginnings filtered into her mind.

The previous day, after a morning in town, Ginny noticed Frank's vehicle parked in Kirk's driveway. With thoughts of her mother overdoing things and what she'd forgotten to buy in the supermarket, it took a few seconds to recognise Mrs Coonan's old place, the appearance was so different. Someone had cleared the overgrown shrubbery, mown the lawns and trimmed the Lilli Pilli hedge along the front fence, reducing it from a rambling mess over three metres high, to a neat—if rather spartan–barrier. The shabby but cute cottage with its wrought-iron trim along the veranda, was once again visible from the road.

Thoughts jumbled through her mind. Maybe that was the reason Kirk hadn't come to Featherwood Station again? He and Frank had been working together on the cottage yard. Or perhaps he'd been working longer days than expected and Frank had taken pity on him?

While visions of the man refused to leave her, she returned her focus to the farm and steeled herself for one of the jobs she disliked most—trucking the yearlings into the saleyards. After rearing them to adulthood, seeing the robust cattle trotting up the saleyard race, confused and bellowing never failed to bring a lump to her throat.

She sighed. Knowing there was no escape from the hard-hitting jobs if the farm was to remain viable, she changed into her oldest jeans and stained shirt and headed to the machinery shed. Remembering the methodical way Lyndon had shown her how, she greased the truck, checked the tyre pressures and batteries, and drove the thirty-year old Isuzu to the end of her road and back to ensure everything was in working order. Then she reversed it into the machinery shed again and headed inside to ring the stock agent and book the sale cattle in, and take a long, hot shower.

The following Sunday, Ginny saddled Akela and prepared to muster cattle for Tuesday's sale. With the dogs trotting behind them, she avoided the granite hill, riding an extra two kilometres through more gentle land instead, until she reached the far corner of the farm. Having spent the previous months in bush-clad hill country, laced with plentiful, protein rich grass, the young cattle were looking better than Ginny had hoped. She was determined to walk them to the yards via the dreaded cutting, but now she jibbed. Except for the day she and Drum had bravely done their investigation, she had taken care to avoid the route. Heat flushed through her as dread filled her insides. She unzipped her jacket, allowing the chilly wind to cool her and squared her shoulders.

The cattle were skittish, frisking and bucking their way around the paddock while the kelpies raced in all directions, desperate to gain control. Ginny sent Flute to the front of the mob to slow them and control the leaders as they neared the track that lead over the hill. In the distance, the massive rocks loomed and butterflies performed ballet inside Ginny's stomach.

Flute trotted ahead, leading the now subdued bovines up the incline. Hooves clattered on the smooth granite rocks as Banjo, Harp and Chime circled the herd continuously, keeping them in a tight mob and forcing them through the narrow opening and down the other side toward the yards.

With Drum hanging behind Akela's heels, Ginny glanced left and right after passing through the cutting, exhaling slowly as she followed the mob into the large holding yard.

While they were relatively meek, she moved them into the smaller yard and then, one by one, pushed them onto the scales, recorded their weight and scanned their ear tag. Then she released them, dividing them into two separate pens—one for the saleable cattle and the other for those who would need to be fed a little longer.

By dusk, she was exhausted but elation drove her on.

I'll take a truckload tomorrow and the balance next week. The remainder could wait until spring. She dragged several bales of hay from the nearby shed and threw them to the cattle before riding Akela back to the stables, unsaddling her and rubbing her down. Then she walked to house, collected the keys for the truck and drove it to the yards, reversing it into the loading ramp in readiness for the following day.

After feeding the menagerie of animals, she topped up the wood box and squatted on the hearth rug. Waiting for the woodchips to catch in the fire, she poked the embers and sat back on her heels as flames licked the pyramid of kindling.

'Now it's my turn—and if the phone rings, I won't answer.' She smiled at the cats as they stretched out on the rug and proceeded to clean themselves, then shuffled to the bathroom and ran herself a deep, hot, bubble bath.

~

On Monday afternoon, as soon as she had finished lunch, Ginny loaded ten of the cattle destined for sale and slid the back gate of the truck closed, dropped the bolts through their cylinders and rubbed her filthy hands down her jeans. The truck rocked as cattle stomped impatiently inside the crate, their hooves clattering on the steel floor.

She climbed into the cab, switched on the engine, and drew slowly away from the loading ramp.

An hour later, she reversed into the dock at the saleyards and slithered out of the truck, greeted by the stock agent.

'Gidday Ginny. Thought you'd be here around now. Any trouble?' The stout, red-faced man pushed his hat toward the back of his head and scratched his thinning scalp.

'No, all good thanks.'

Alan had been Lyndon and Ginny's stock agent for over twenty years and, when Ginny had phoned him to book the cattle in, had offered to come to Featherwood Station and help. However, Ginny had refused, determined to cope alone—but had allowed herself two days to complete what had taken less than one when Lyndon was alive, just in case.

Beside them, a massive stock truck beeped rhythmically as it reversed into the ramp, a hiss of airbrakes announcing mission accomplished.

Ginny handed Alan her waybill and they moved to the rear of the truck as a yardman approached.

'This lot ready to go?' The man yelled over the racket of cattle bellowing, truck engines and the ring of hooves.

'Yep!' Alan replied and Ginny unbolted the rear sliding door.

Within seconds the cattle were out and trotting up the race toward an overnight yard.

'You're right to go now Ginny. Leave the rest to us.' Alan said kindly before swinging his attention to the paperwork in his hand.

'Righto. See you next week with another load.'

With a brief wave, the agent hurried away and Ginny climbed back into the driver's seat and drove onto the main road.

In comparison to the trip to the saleyards, the homeward journey was always easy. With an empty truck and the majority of the roads either flat or on a downhill slope, the well-used vehicle trundled along at a comfortable pace.

At the top of the hill descending into Featherwood Falls, Ginny hummed to herself and changed down a gear—just as a kangaroo leapt out of the roadside scrub and bounded across in front of her. She slammed her foot on the brake. Tyres squealed as the animal leapt into the bush.

'Phew. That was close.' She accelerated and changed up a gear. As the momentum increased on the downhill run, she rested her foot lightly on the brake. It resisted for a split second before the pedal slowly dropped to the floor. She gasped, panic crushing her chest and pumped the brake again. With no resistance, instead of slowing, the vehicle increased speed as it faced the steep slope.

Terror filled Ginny as she pumped frantically. Nothing. She slammed her left foot on the clutch and wrestled the lever. Cogs crunched, preventing access to a lower gear. A loud scraping noise filled the cab and the truck swayed. Realising the use of lower gears to slow the vehicle was impossible, Ginny forced it into a higher gear and hauled on the hand brake. No match against the combined speed and truck weight, Ginny continued to stamp the foot pedal furiously while her pulse pounded in her ears.

Trees passed in a blur, while visions of the truck overturning in the table drain or crashing into an oncoming vehicle filled Ginny with alarm. She rocketed past the turnoff to her property, desperately grasping the hand brake with her left hand while she gripped the steering wheel in her right. In a final attempt to slow the truck, she swung the wheel hard, forcing the vehicle off the road through a row of shrubs and onto the thick grass next to the local park.

As it slowed to a halt, Ginny switched the ignition off and slumped over the steering wheel. It seemed like an age but may have been only seconds before a shout carried through the air. She looked up to see a white-faced Frank running toward her. His hat flew off as he ran, his uneven gait slowing as he reached for the handle and wrenched the door open.

'Are you alright? What the hell happened?'

Frozen with shock, Ginny barely registered his brisk assessment of her body, even when running his hand over her jean-clad legs. Laying his hand on her arm, his kind voice finally registered.

'It's okay, love. You're not hurt. Do you feel well enough to get out?'

Ginny obeyed, slithering onto the ground where she crumpled in a heap. She looked up at him numbly.

Squatting beside her, he patted her shoulder and waited.

'The brakes failed, Frank.' Her voice was a thin whisper. 'I thought I'd checked everything but I never considered the brakes failing. Should I have done more?'

'Don't worry, love. I'll have a look for you and see if we can find where the problem is. At least you're safe —and you even managed to save the rusty old girl.' He gave her a wink and grinned, easing Ginny's shock. 'Do you think you can walk over to the store?'

She nodded and rose to her feet. Tucking her arm in his, Frank led her to where Lola was dashing across the grass toward them.

'Oh Ginny. I'm pleased to see you're alright. What happened? We heard the truck screaming down the hill and thought it was one of those overloaded road trains trying to avoid the Main Road's inspectors by taking the back roads.' She grasped Ginny's other arm and they escorted her up the steps and into the kitchen.

'While you get a good cup of tea into her, I'll have a look at those brakes,' Frank said.

Ginny nodded silently and fixed her gaze on Lola as she boiled the kettle and made two cups of sweetened tea.

'Here, get this inside you.' Lola pushed the mug toward Ginny, a worried frown spreading across her forehead. 'Dear God. You were lucky.'

'I seem jinxed, don't I?'

Lola jumped up and wrapped her arms around Ginny's shoulders. 'No, love. You're just overworked and trying too hard to be independent.'

While Ginny regained her composure in her friend's company, she cursed herself for not ordering a carrier to take the cattle instead of trying to follow in Lyndon's footsteps. *I might have reduced the costs but at least I wouldn't be in this predicament now.*

The bell tinkled and Frank entered the kitchen, wiping his hands on a rag. His already wrinkled face appeared even more weather-beaten than usual as creases etched deep in his forehead.

'I'm gonna give Warren a ring.'

Lola jerked her head toward her husband, a worried expression covering her face. 'Why?'

'I'm not happy about those brakes.' He looked at Ginny with concern. 'Has anyone been around your place lately?'

Ginny's eyes widened. 'I don't think so. Not in the last month anyway. Who is Warren?'

'A mate who runs a mobile mechanical business. He's semi-retired these days but I'm sure he'll be able to pop out and have a look. I might be over-reacting and I admit I'm not a mechanic, but, to me, the brake line appears to have been interfered with.'

'What!' Ginny paled as bile burned the back of her throat. 'Not again.'

Frank pulled out the chair next to her and sat, leaning forward, his face only a metre from hers. 'What is this about—not again.' Has this happened before?'

She shook her head. 'No, I'm sorry. I don't mean the truck brakes. It's just … well, so many things have been going wrong lately. The windmill, the attempted fire, the cattle being mixed up.' She stopped, suddenly aware of Frank and Lola's intense attention.

'I think you'd better tell us everything.' Frank leaned back and Lola squirmed in her seat, as though making herself more comfortable.

Ginny began hesitantly—apologetically–as though convincing herself she was somehow at fault.

Fifteen minutes later, she finished. Her shoulders slumped as the realisation set in. 'You believe me don't you?'

Lola covered her hand with her own. 'Of course we do, love. I can't understand why Stan doesn't though.'

Frank harrumphed. 'I do. In his eyes there's no evidence to prove it wasn't Ginny's forgetfulness, and even if there was a shred of proof it wasn't her fault, he'd be too lazy to follow it up ... unless something really bad does happen and he is forced to.' He glanced at Ginny, his lips pressed into a tight, flat line.

'That's enough now. Frank, you stay here and look after the shop and I'll run Ginny home,' Lola ordered.

Powerless, Ginny dragged herself to her feet and followed her friend to the back door as Frank called, 'Don't worry about the truck, Ginny. I'll look after it and once Warren's checked it out, I'll get him to repair any damage and bring it to you.'

A shudder crept over her as she stepped outside, flinching as Bert, Lola's rescued Cockatoo squawked loudly, breaking into her thoughts.

Am I going mad? What if I did forget about the wind-mill—and the gates? She lifted her gaze and stared at the familiar square-fronted truck sitting forlornly by the park. *No matter what they think, if the brakes were tampered with, then I know that someone wants me gone.*

20

The following morning, Ginny looked up with surprise as an unfamiliar, battered Hino truck crawled down her drive toward her.

Hesitantly, she pushed the gate open and stood, waiting. Frank lowered himself from the passenger's seat while a withered man with a shock of white hair stepped onto the dirt. He approached her with a wide smile and an outstretched hand.

'Warren Butler.'

She returned his smile and squeezed his work-roughened hand, her breath hitching.

'Did you find the problem?' she asked.

Warren took a deep breath and gave a slight shake of his head. 'Yes, I'm afraid I did—and it's not what you'll be wanting to hear.'

Ginny straightened, her hands dropping to her sides as the emptiness inside her grew.

'And?'

'I'm afraid it might be time to call the police. There's no doubt someone has tampered with your brakes. Premeditated, I'd say, judging by their actions.'

'So you're quite sure it couldn't have been neglect on my part?'

Warren shook his head again and glanced at Frank whose normally crinkled, happy face was solemn and pale.

'Frank said you'd taken the truck for a run only a couple of days beforehand. Were the brakes working alright then?'

Ginny cleared her throat, her mouth dry. 'I'm sure of it. I didn't go far—only to the end of the road and back, and I didn't go down the hill so I guess I didn't have to brake hard. But I did use them before turning and then again after backing into the loading ramp at the yards.' She rubbed her cheeks with the palms of her hands, revisiting every move of the exercise. 'I did everything Lyndon taught me—only because it had been a couple of months since I last drove it–and then decided to put it in position for loading the cattle to save myself the job on Monday.'

'Well ... it seems to me that someone didn't want you to make that trip—or perhaps they didn't want you to come home again. Either way, there's no doubt you've been targeted—with a one sixteenth diameter drill bit and insulation tape by the look of it.'

Ginny reached for the gate post and clung to it as she processed Warren's information. 'Would you be prepared to put your opinion in writing?'

He nodded. 'Of course. You'll need to report it to your local copper—and I'm happy to give him a call myself if you like?'

Frank stepped closer to Ginny. 'How about I come with you to see Stan?'

She ran a jerky hand through her hair and swallowed. 'Thanks Frank. I'd appreciate that. Should we go now?'

'I reckon so. Get it over with as soon as possible so he can get off his lazy backside and do his job.'

'Right. I'll just grab my car keys and lock up.'

'Warren, I'll go with Ginny if that's okay with you? See you down there?'

Warren nodded silently at both Frank and Ginny and climbed back into his truck.

WITH HIS FEET on the desk and a half empty cup of coffee in his hand, Stan appeared to be engrossed in a book when they pushed the station door open and trooped inside.

He lowered his legs slowly and pushed himself to his feet, a nonchalant smirk touching his mouth.

'Well, well. Three visitors at the same time looks a bit serious.'

'Yeah. You're aware Ginny's had a few concerns on the station of late?' Frank said.

Under Stan's gaze, Ginny crossed her arms over her chest and swallowed.

'Oh yeah, the windmill that wasn't pumping,' Stan brushed crumbs from his chest before leaning his elbows on the counter. 'Don't tell me it's misbehaving again?'

Ginny squared her shoulders. 'No Stan. It's a bit more serious this time. I had a mishap yesterday in the truck. Warren here has inspected it and has discovered a very concerning issue.' She tipped her head at her companions. Frank stepped forward, leaning directly opposite Stan, meeting him eye for eye.

'Someone tampered with the brakes on Ginny's truck—and this time, I'd like to think you'll take the information seriously.'

'I see.' Stan's eyes widened. Moving toward the door into a side office, he opened it and beckoned them in.'

'Have a seat.'

Chairs scraped and papers rustled as they settled themselves around the solid, timber desk.

With a blasé shrug, Stan jotted their names, date,

and time at the top of the report before leaning back in his chair. Then, with his pen poised, he met Ginny's stare. 'Righto Ginny, let's get as much information down as you can give me.'

She detailed her maintenance check, the trip to the saleyards and then the terrifying moment when, on the descent to the turn into her road, the brakes refused to operate.

She twisted her fingers together as she finished, her heart racing.

'Righto. And you, Warren? You're a qualified diesel mechanic I gather?' Stan asked.

'Correct. I have inspected the truck thoroughly at Frank's request, and my findings were very concerning.'

'I see. In what way?'

'I noticed a piece of tape wrapped around the brake line. One end had blown off, I suspect when Ginny pumped the brake hard coming down the hill. Anyhow, underneath that tape, was a small hole. Looks to me as though it was made with a fine drill bit—but no doubt your forensic team will confirm that.' Warren's tone was firm and factual and his eyes never left Stan's.

Pausing for a moment, Stan squinted before scribbling furiously on the sheet in front of him.

'Anything else any of you'd like to add?' he asked.

Frank leaned forward. 'I heard the truck screaming

down the hill as I was around the side chopping wood. As soon as I saw it emerge from behind the trees, I knew it was Ginny's and that she was in trouble.'

'I see.'

Frank looked at Ginny again. 'That would have been when you made the decision to get off the road and onto the park?'

'Yes.' She nodded. 'It happened so quickly, I only remember seeing the electricity pole flash past and I knew that if I didn't get off the road where the table drain flattened out, I'd either end up rolling, or worse still, collide with something, or someone, in my path.'

'Hmm. Very brave of you it turns out—I guess it was a good thing you knew the road, and the verges, so well.' Stan sniffed and finished the report, requested their signatures, and pushed his chair back. 'Do you have any idea who might be responsible for this—or any reason why anyone would want to hurt you?'

She shook her head. 'None.'

'Where's the truck now?' he asked.

'Still in the park where we stopped yesterday evening.' Ginny said.

'Right. I'll let head office know about this and arrange to have it shifted to our holding yard, Ginny. I expect the forensic officer will want to give it a thorough going-over—and I'll give you a ring to let you know when to expect them. Who's got the keys?'

Frank fished them out of his pocket and handed them over.

Grateful that Stan appeared to have taken her incident seriously, Ginny breathed a sigh of relief and shot him a warm smile. Outside again, she faced Frank and then Warren.

'Thanks so much. I appreciate your support—and your mechanical expertise, Warren. I think Stan understood my concern this time.'

Frank harrumphed. 'I hope so, love. It's not right. This community hasn't had problems for years—well, except for the odd illegal drug plantation or two. The last thing we need is someone making trouble—and frightening one of our Featherwood Falls family.'

Ginny repeated her thanks, her lip quivering. 'Can I drop you at the shop, Frank?'

'Thanks for the offer, love, but no. Warren and I thought we'd have a quiet beer together. You're very welcome to join us of course?'

She chuckled. 'Thanks for the invitation—but I think after all that's happened, I just want my own home and a good cup of tea.' Lifting one hand in a brief wave, she fished her keys out of her jeans pocket with the other and headed for the car.

~

SUNSHINE ENCOMPASSED the north facing veranda and Ginny wandered into its warmth, her hands wrapped around her mug. She lifted the cat from its curled position in the cane lounge chair and nestled herself into the vacant spot, lowering the limp, half-asleep body onto her lap. A deep rumble emitted from the tabby and she smiled, stroking Kimba gently, while Flute curled up at her feet.

With her mug empty, she leaned back, her head resting on the plump, softness of the chair's cushioned lining and closed her eyes.

She must have dozed and woke with a start at the sound of Flute's warning bark and a vehicle approaching. The sun had moved and she shivered in the pool of shade. Lifting the cat, she stood up, placed Kimba back on the chair and peered through the lattice at the end of the veranda.

Her heart skipped. 'Kirk?'

With long strides, his tall, handsome frame reached the gate before she did. He smiled, a wide, all embracing smile that emphasized his straight white teeth and dark beard.

'Gidday.'

Her breath caught and she hesitated for a split second before reaching out and grasping his outstretched hand, pulling him gently through the gate.

'Hi. It's good to see you. Come in?'

'Love to. Work's been a bit full on the last few weeks and, as we finished early today, I thought it was time I paid a visit to my neighbour.'

The smile hadn't left his face and she beamed at him.

'I'll put the kettle on—or would you like something a bit stronger?'

'Tea's fine.' He looked at his watch. 'Probably a bit early to start on the hard stuff, don't you think?'

She giggled and flicked her hair out of her face. 'Tea it is then.'

While the kettle boiled, Kirk lowered himself onto a dining chair and watched as Ginny made the tea and laid melting moments on a plate.

'Yum. One of my favourites.' He pointed to the cream, shortcake biscuits sandwiching pink icing in between them. 'Homemade I presume?'

'Of course. I don't bake as frequently as I used to—with only me here, I don't need them. But ... being able to freeze most things means that at least I can offer my visitors something delicious when they visit.'

'Well, I'm pleased. So ... what have you been doing lately?'

Ginny sighed. 'How long have you got?'

'Oh. That sounds ominous.' He straightened, his eyes narrowing. 'Something wrong?'

Ginny poured out the story of mustering the cattle, the trip to the saleyards and the frightening journey home. Kirk sat in silence, his jaw dropping when she got to Warren's discovery. He reached out his hand and squeezed hers.

'Are you okay?'

'Yes, I'm fine ... although I didn't sleep much last night.'

'I'm not surprised. When is the forensic guy coming to have a look?'

Ginny shrugged. 'Not sure. Stan said he'd arrange for the truck to be taken to the police holding yard, neat the station to be held for examination. He will notify the appropriate sections. I guess it could be any time?'

Kirk rested his arms on the table and leaned forward. 'I've been putting in some long hours for Neil lately—and we've made great progress. I'm sure he wouldn't mind if I took a few days off and hung around here for a bit ... just to make sure you're safe of course.'

She shot him a quick grin. 'Thanks. You don't have to do that though. I'll be fine. Flute's keeping me company now and I'll let the other dogs take turns joining her in the house yard each night, just in case.'

He stroked his beard, his eyes full of shadows. 'I've been thinking about the renovations to your quarters —for the farm stay thing–and wondered if you'd like me to put a kitchen in where you had planned?'

Ginny blinked. 'Really?'

'Well—if the building was ready for visitors, as

soon as people start travelling again, perhaps you could open up. At least then you wouldn't be alone here—and you might get a bit of help now and then around the place.'

'It's a good thought.' Ginny shook her head. 'I'm sorry, I don't seem to be able to think that far ahead at the moment.' She blew out a deep breath and grimaced. 'The events around here lately have rattled me and ... well, I'm not sure what to do. Wait until the cops have been and done their investigation first, I guess.'

'I understand. No pressure. I've got a few more weeks to hang around before it's warm enough for me to head for the hills, so I'm happy to help out if you'd like me to.'

The phone rang.

'This could be important. Do you mind if I get that?'

He nodded and she picked up the handpiece.

'Hello?'

'Mrs Shepherd?' A deep, solemn voice resonated down the line.

'Yes.'

'Sergeant Robert Malcolm, from the Warwick Scenes of Crime Office. I've examined your truck and would like to visit your property to inspect the area where your truck was parked please?'

'Oh! Of-of course,' she stuttered. 'Now?'

'Yes. I'll be there within twenty minutes.'

'Oh, okay. See you soon.' She hung up and relayed the message to Kirk.

A brief, relieved smile lit up his face. 'Good.' He paused for a moment. 'You mentioned you've got another load of cattle to get into the saleyards next week. I think it would be a good idea if you organised a carrier for them. I have my doubts that you'll have this vehicle ready to use by then—even if you want to.'

'Good idea. Thanks. I'll ring and book him now.'

'While you're doing that, do you mind if I have another look at the quarters? I'd like to get a feel for what needs to be done.' He shot her an apologetic smile. 'I know it's too much for you to think about at the moment, but I'd like to help—and if I can get the place rentable, I'll have the satisfaction of knowing you'll have people coming and going and won't be alone as often.'

'Thanks Kirk.' Ginny smiled, unaware of the effect her smile had on him.

She watched him stride toward the quarters for a minute before returning to the house to make the phone call. For the first time since Lyndon's death, the hollow emptiness that sat inside her dissipated and she smiled.

'With you here, I feel safe,' she whispered.

21

*E*xactly twenty minutes later, a Police Hilux pulled up outside the house and a tall, lean man in dark blue Police overalls stepped out. Ginny hurried to meet him.

'Mrs Shepherd?' He asked, keeping his distance, and removed a handkerchief from his pocket and proceeded to clean his black rimmed glasses.

'Yes. I'm Ginny.'

'Sergeant Robert Malcolm.' He cleared his throat. 'We spoke on the phone. Would you mind showing me where the truck was parked prior to your trip to town?'

She nodded. 'It usually lives in the machinery shed here.' She indicated the huge shed fifty metres away. 'But, on Saturday, I checked it over and then drove it to the yards in readiness for loading the cattle on Monday.'

'And how far away are the yards?'

'Over the hill behind the house—about half a kilo-metre or so.'

'Okay. Jump in. We'll drive there if you don't mind.'

Following his instructions, Ginny climbed into the Hilux and directed the officer through the open gate onto the track leading directly to the yards.

At the site, he took several photos, peered closely at the ground around the loading ramp, and frowned.

'Looks like boot marks here—and a smoothed patch of damp soil, as though someone has lain on the ground.'

Ginny's eyes widened.

'I'll get a magnet. See if there's any metal shavings in the area,' he said.

Her curiosity piqued and she followed him from the vehicle back to the area he'd been inspecting so closely.

'Hmm.' He pulled the magnet close to his face, studying it intently. 'As I thought.' Then he returned to the vehicle, extracted a small screw top jar, and handed it to Ginny. 'Would you mind removing the lid please? I'll scrape these into it.'

'W-what does that mean?'

He peered over the top of his glasses, his head tilted and she met his gaze, surprised to note that he probably wasn't as old as she had first thought.

'Time will tell—but there's a good chance these are

the filings from the brake line, indicating someone definitely used a drill to bore a hole here, at this site.'

While Ginny stared, he asked, 'Any men been around this area lately?'

She shook her head. 'No, only me—and my boots are not that big.' She pointed to the clear boot-print in the soil beside the grass.

'I'll take a photograph and cast of the print, and scrapings of that dark patch in the dirt.'

'Oh.' She peered at the small, dark area about the size of a twenty cent piece.

As she watched the officer complete his examination, her heart beat faster. Uneasiness grew inside her. *Who could be doing this to me?*

Robert lifted his gaze and packed his equipment away. 'I'm finished here now. I'll drop you back at the house and you should hear from the CIB within the next day or so.'

'Thanks.'

The short journey back to the house was completed in silence as Ginny's mind raced.

The vehicle came to a halt and she slid out, repeating her thanks once again.

A shout stopped her from heading inside and she turned to see Kirk striding toward her from the quarters. She waved, relief flooding through her. Reaching for the gate, she leaned heavily on it, rubbed the sweat from her forehead on her sleeve and waited until the dizziness passed. Her chin trembled as Kirk reached her and, without a word, he wrapped his arms around her.

His warmth was reinforced by the scent of spicy aftershave and Ginny leaned into him without hesitation. Pressed against his chest, she felt small ... and safe.

They remained in each other's arms for a long minute before he spoke.

'Pretty rough, hey?'

She breathed deeply, stepped back, and looked into his eyes. 'You could say that.'

'Did the forensic guy find anything?'

'Yes. Evidence of someone lying on the ground where the truck was parked—and metal shavings supporting the use of a drill on the brake line. Oh, and he also found a boot print so took a cast of it.'

'Wow!' Kirk's face was solemn but impassive.

He reached for the gate, keeping his arm around her, and guided her into the house.

'I don't think I should leave you.' His forehead creased as she slumped into the chair.

Attempting a grin, she shrugged. 'It's okay, Kirk. I'm just a bit shocked I guess. Not really what you expect in a friendly little backwater like Featherwood Falls.'

'I agree.' His face wore a pensive look as he stroked his beard.

In an attempt to shift her focus from the whole

truck incident, Ginny asked. 'What did you think of the quarters?'

He blinked as if having forgotten about his inspection.

'Oh. It looks great—and putting in a corner kitchen on one end of the veranda will be straightforward and shouldn't take long at all. With the plumbing already set up for the bathroom, we can get a plumber to rough everything in, then I can do the tidying up and installation and he only needs to come back and sign off on it all. That's if you want me too, of course?'

She gave him a wan smile and shrugged. 'I'd love you too.'

Outside, dusk was falling and Kirk got up and switched on the light.

'So ... would you like me to stay?'

Heat flushed up her neck. *What did he mean exactly?* She froze, her heart toying with her head.

'Thanks for the offer, Kirk. But no. I'll be okay—I've got the dogs with me and I suspect that whoever did this already knows the police are onto it. Hopefully that will be enough for them to lie low ... for a while anyway.' Her voice shook and she cleared her throat.

He ran his hand lightly over her hair and nodded.

'Okay. I'm just down the road if you need me. I know we haven't got mobile coverage here but you could turn on the outside lights and toot your car horn a few times. I'm a light sleeper and I'm pretty sure I'd hear that.'

She chuckled. 'Yeah, you and half the valley I suspect.'

Standing on tip-toes, she kissed his cheek before stepping back hastily.

He hesitated, sharing a smile, and moved toward the door. 'I'll pop up in the morning to check on you— if that's alright?'

'I'd appreciate that. Thanks. I know Lola would come and stay the night with me if I get really worried.'

It was too soon to consider allowing Kirk—or any other man for that matter–to stay in the house with her, regardless of what her body was suggesting.

She looked down, unable to meet his eyes as she studied his enormous boots.

'Righto. See you tomorrow then,' he replied softly. And then he was gone.

As DARKNESS FELL, Ginny switched on all the indoor lights, restless and anxious. Unable to settle in the eerily quiet house, she faced Oscar's questioning gaze.

'I'm not going to let this get to me.'

Then she wrapped herself in her warmest jacket, slipped a thermos of tea, a torch, and a sandwich in her backpack and locked the doors. Striding to the kennels with Flute and Drum at her feet, she opened the gates of the remaining three dog pens, allowing Banjo, Harp and Chime to leap out in a tumble of joy.

'Come on. We're going to the waterfall to watch the moon rise.'

Wearing a head-torch to light the way, they climbed the ridge in the half dark. By the time they reached the waterfall, she was puffing heavily and she stood quietly to regain her breath. After recent rain, it had swollen and the rushing water rang over the rocks, bubbling and churning noisily.

Perching on a rock far enough away from the waterfall so as to not get wet, she stretched out her legs and let her eyes adjust to the growing darkness. Shifting position, she stamped her feet to keep her warm as the cold bit and consumed her sandwich and two mugs full of hot tea. Almost an hour later, the light changed, the moon rose into view and the valley was bathed in silver light. Shadows surrounded Nigel's packing shed while, in Featherwood Falls, the four street lamps melted into soft yellow specks, barely discernible in the moonlight.

She breathed the cold air, smiling at the clouds of steam that she puffed out. Flute and Drum pressed their warm bodies against hers and she lay an arm over each of them.

Uninhabited for almost two years, a light now twinkled from Mrs Coonan's cottage. Ginny's chest tightened. She wondered what Kirk was thinking, the urge to rush home and jump in the car to ask him to stay with her, strong.

Resisting the temptation, she continued to sit until her bottom was numb and the dogs restlessly began to nudge her.

'Alright. Time to go home.' She repacked her bag and strapped it onto her back before fastening the head torch around her forehead. Then, with the dogs leading the way, she trekked back to the house. She fed and locked Harp, Chime and Drum in their pens before calling Flute and Banjo to follow her into the house yard.

After a hot shower, Ginny curled up on the couch in front of the fire and switched the television on. The phone rang just as she got settled and she groaned.

'Hello?' She took the handpiece back to the couch with her and pulled a rug over her legs.

'Virginia. It's Donald.'

Ginny's lips formed a thin line. *What do you want?*

'I heard your cattle sold well.'

Ginny gasped, clenching her jaw. 'Really? I hadn't heard.'

A confident laugh echoed down the phone and she felt her blood pressure rising.

'Yeah. I was at the sale this morning. Thought you would have been there too, seeing as you had cattle to sell.'

'I had other things to do.' She bit her lip in a desperate attempt to prevent her annoyance from escalating.

'Good money. Well done you.'

'Thank you, Donald.' Silence reigned for a few seconds and she pointed the remote at the television and turned the volume down. 'Was there something else?'

'Have you given any more thought to letting me buy Featherwood Station from you?'

Frustration rose in Ginny and she retorted, 'Donald. I will not be selling the property to you, or anyone else for that matter. I thought I had made that quite clear.'

'Andrew thought you might have changed your mind after the cattle mix-up.'

Ginny froze. 'How did you know about that?'

He snorted. 'There's not much I don't know. You'd be surprised how news travels so quickly.'

Suddenly, nausea filled Ginny and she tucked her shaking hand under the blanket.

'In that case, I'm assuming you know about the sabotage to my truck?'

His reply was smooth—so even that Ginny couldn't decide if he knew something or was bluffing.

'This and that. Probably something a bit of maintenance would have prevented. These are the reasons I'm serious about buying the property. It's too much for you—that's quite obvious.'

'Good night, Donald.' Ginny pressed the red button and threw the phone to the end of the couch.

'How dare he.'

Her anger escalated. She tossed the blanket aside and paced up and down the hallway, her thoughts tumbling in her head. Was Donald responsible for the incidents that had been occurring? Could he and Andrew be hatching a plan to get her off—so Donald could become "Lord of the Manor"?

'No!' Her outburst startled Flute who crept across the floor to stare anxiously at her mistress.

Dropping to her knees, Ginny wrapped her arms around the little dog and lay her face on her neck.

'It's okay, little one.'

She sat beside the dog for several minutes, stroking her smooth coat and breathing steadily. As her pulse returned to normal, she glanced at the clock. Ten-fifteen.

'Time for bed, I think,' she said to Flute. 'And tonight, you're allowed to sleep beside me.'

22

*A*s good as his word, Kirk arrived at seven-thirty the following morning.

Fog hung in the valley, blanketing all signs of civilisation. In Ginny's garden, trees and shrubs dripped moisture and all around them, the frosty air was whisper quiet.

Ginny was feeding the chooks when she heard the vehicle's distinctive rumble. In the misty gloom, she was unsure if it was approaching, or leaving? She closed the hen-house door and hurried to the house.

Her heart leapt at the sight of the vehicle parked beside the gate and she called out.

'I'm here, Kirk!'

He strode toward her and gave her a quick hug.

'Have you had breakfast?' she asked.

He grinned. 'Not yet. Just coffee. Thought I'd check on things here first.'

'Come on then. I'll cook us both a decent meal.'

A few minutes later, the smells of cooked bacon and coffee drifted through the house. While Kirk buttered toast, Ginny dropped eggs into the pan, her fears easing as her stomach rumbled with hunger.

It didn't take long to demolish every mouthful and Ginny sat back in her chair, satiated, and feeling stronger and more positive than she had the previous evening. Bending to feed Flute a piece of bacon-rind, she grinned at Kirk's sock encased feet. *I thought so—much too big.*

She was carrying their empty plates to the sink when the phone rang.

'Leave those to me while you answer that,' Kirk said.

She grinned at him and picked up the receiver.

'Hello?'

'Hello. Mrs Shepherd?'

'Yes.'

'Detective Senior Constable James Avery from Warwick Police Station. I've been detailed the investigation relating to what happened with your truck. Is this a good time to talk?'

The Detective confirmed her address and estimated time of his arrival before hanging up.

She met Kirk's enquiring gaze as her stomach twisted with anxiety again.

'That was the Detective. They're on their way out to have a look at the truck—and to talk to me.

GINNY CLASPED her fingers so tightly together that her knuckles shone white. Too shocked to move, she stared at the kind face of the Detective.

'It certainly looks as though you're the target—for whatever reason.'

'But why?' she whispered.

'That's over to us to find out. We're taking this matter very seriously. The act has definitely been deliberate and has had a lot of thought put into it. The question remaining is did someone intend to harm you? Or just frighten you? So ... as you can appreciate, the offenses we are looking at range from attempted murder to an act endangering life.'

Ginny sucked in a sudden breath, her eyes wide.

'The forensic examination has revealed whoever interfered with your braking system was wearing gloves.' He looked around the room. 'Do you live alone?'

Ginny nodded. 'Yes, my husband died in an accident almost sixteen months ago now and both my daughters live elsewhere—one in Scotland and one in

Sydney–and haven't been able to come home because of the pandemic.'

'Oh!' Confusion flashed across his face for an instant. 'I assumed the gentleman we met outside, Kirk, was your husband.'

'No. He's a neighbour. Lives down the road.' She squirmed under his questioning gaze. 'He came to Featherwood Falls in April—about a week after Easter I think.'

The Detective scribbled something in his book before tucking the pen in his pocket and rising to his feet. 'I'll be in touch again, Mrs Shepherd. In the meantime, we'll be talking to your neighbours and members of the community. Before I catch up with Kirk, would you mind showing me exactly where the truck was parked?'

'Do you mean where the forensic officer found evidence?'

'Yes. I believe you had done some maintenance on the vehicle beforehand?'

'I checked the oil and tyres on Saturday and then drove it to the cattle yards the following day so it would be ready for me to load the cattle on Monday. I thought it would save me time.'

'I understand. Can you see the cattle yards from the house?'

'No. They're over the other side of the rise—behind a belt of trees.'

He stared at her. 'Hmm. I'd like to take a quick look there if I may—before I talk to your neighbour.'

'Oh. Okay. Do you want me to take you there?'

'If you can direct me, I'm sure I'll find it—and I promise I won't leave any gates open.' He smiled then and she relaxed.

'Thank you Detective.'

'Please, call me James.' He smiled. 'By the way, Senior Constable Brennan told us you'd had another couple of incidents here recently. One involving a kerosene spillage under the woolshed, and the other where someone appears to have tied up your windmill, preventing it from drawing water.'

'Correct.' Unease gnawed at her insides, refusing to dissipate.

As she followed him out the door, she rubbed her upper arms. *Did James think Kirk might be a suspect?* She choked as a laugh rose in her throat. *How ridiculous.*

Deep down, she suspected she was falling in love with the man.

THE INVESTIGATION CONTINUED for days as Ginny made the rounds of feeding hay to the stock, drenching sheep and preparing the balance of the sale cattle for the carrier.

Rain arrived the week after her interview with

James and she trudged around the animals in her oilskin coat and gumboots, slipping in the mud and accumulating a pile of wet, dirty clothes on the laundry floor.

Her confidence grew with almost daily conversations with Lola and her daughters—their support immeasurable.

'You can beat this mongrel, Mum,' Claire said. 'There's talk of the Queensland borders being opened at the beginning of September. If everything is okay down here, I'm coming home.'

'Darling, you don't have to. I'll be fine. The police are working on it and I'm sure that whoever is trying to scare me will be lying low. Anyway, the more they try, the more I'm determined to not give in!' She grinned to herself. 'I've got the truck back and Warren will be here to fix it next week hopefully.'

'Good. I'm still coming home. I've had enough of the city. And one thing we've discovered since all these lock-downs began, way more of us can work from home that we ever imagined.'

Ginny chuckled. 'Alright, I'd love you to be here with me again.' She hesitated. 'Except that you might have to investigate satellite internet or something that connects you to the outside world a bit better than my struggling dongle does.'

"We'll be fine, Mum. You look after yourself and I'll worry about that later.'

Having hidden the list of concerning events from her mother so as not to worry her, Ginny was relieved that the restrictions around visiting the "aged" as the government put it, was now both permitted and the right time for her to pay her a visit. It was one thing to share just enough without frightening her—and quite another if she was to hear an exaggerated version from someone else.

She changed into a pair of black trousers, cream cashmere jumper and a rich, copper coloured jacket. Then, adding knee-length boots and a bright, autumn toned scarf, she applied makeup and brushed her hair until it shone in bouncy waves around her shoulders.

Adding a container of biscuits from the freezer and a jar of home-made tomato chutney to her basket, she swung her leather handbag over her shoulder and locked the door.

After the previous day's deluge, the sky was clear— a vivid blue, dotted with an occasional fluffy white cloud. Ginny turned up the volume on the car radio and sang along to Queen's Bohemian Rhapsody as she drove.

'Ginny! I didn't know you were coming today?'

She hugged the frail frame of her mother and smiled. 'Sorry mum. It was a spur of the moment thing. With the farm work, and then the rain ... you know, I felt like I needed to get away for a few hours.'

'Well. It's lovely to see you.' She turned toward the

immaculate town house porch and opened the screen door. 'Come in. I'll put the kettle on.'

Love for her mother washed over Ginny and she sighed. After her father died six years earlier, her mother had been in shock for weeks. Ginny had often wished she hadn't been an only child. Having siblings might have relieved the guilt—the sense of responsibility that she felt for her aging mother. But, she sighed, she'd had no control over that issue and had been relieved when her mother morphed from a devoted housewife to a social butterfly, revelling in joining every committee she could and learning how to operate her brand new iPad. Ginny glanced at the array of photos on the sideboard and a soft smile rested on her lips. Her parents wedding, the three of them when Ginny was a tiny baby, Ginny at around twelve, hugging her first dog, a Cavalier King Charles Spaniel she'd called Lady, after one of her favourite childhood books "Lady and the Tramp". Additional photos of her and Lyndon's wedding, the girls as babies, school girls and then in their formal dresses.

'Here you go, love.' Mavis placed a delicate, bone-china teapot on the round dining table before setting up two cups, saucers, and plates. A flute-edged cake plate came next before she removed the lid from Ginny's biscuits and spread them on it.

A few minutes later, with their cups empty and the

exchange of family news and idle gossip dealt with, Ginny drew a deep breath.

'Mum, I've got something to tell you.' Mavis raised her face and stared at her daughter, her eyes wide.

'You're not pregnant?'

Ginny choked on a giggle and her mother smiled.

'No, of course not.' She fiddled with her cup, turning it in circles on the saucer. 'It's a bit more serious than that I'm afraid.'

Mavis narrowed her eyes. 'Well, you'd better tell me then.'

Ginny chose her words carefully, wary of upsetting her mother. Glossing over the kerosene tin occurrence with minimum detail, she shared the issue with the windmill, laughingly attributing it to her forgetfulness. When she downloaded the more serious incident with the trucks brakes, her mother clapped a hand over her mouth.

'So the police are involved?'

'Yes. They're looking into it ... because there's a chance it wasn't a maintenance problem. They seem to think I've been targeted.'

Mavis slumped in her chair, her eyes wide. 'Oh my goodness. This is like an Agatha Christie story.'

'Well—not quite, Mum. I don't want you to worry because the police have got everything under control. I just didn't want you hearing gossip from someone and not understanding what's been going on.'

'Of course. At least you're not sick or anything—that would be awful.' Ginny blinked as her mother continued. 'Are you safe? I mean—do they really think someone is trying to frighten you? If they are, who is it and why?'

Ginny shrugged and attempted to quell the rising panic welling up inside her. Even talking about it again brought her fears to the fore—and she had to hide that from her mother at all costs.

'We don't know. And maybe we never will—but I assure you I'm safe. I have a new neighbour living close by and Frank and Lola phone or call in almost every day. Anyway, I've got the dogs, and even the local cop is now ringing to check on me every so often.' She reached out and squeezed her mother's hand. 'Don't worry. It'll all be sorted out soon, I'm sure.'

'If you say so, dear.' Mavis gathered up the cups and carried them to the bench. 'Come and have a look at my Hellebores. Their flowers are so beautiful this year.'

Ginny let her shoulders drop, the hint of a smile tipping her lips. It seemed that even bad news couldn't ruffle this old girl.

23

*T*wo weeks went by with no further contact from James and, fed up with waiting, Ginny picked up the phone.

'Detective Senior Constable James Avery.'

'Hello James. It's Ginny Shepherd.'

'How are you Ginny?'

'Well thanks. I was wondering how the investigation is going. Any news?'

James cleared his throat and the sound of papers shuffling filled the following seconds.

'We've done a door knock around your neighbours and in the Featherwood community—to see if anyone else has experienced anything unusual. Unfortunately ... or perhaps fortunately, it seems you're the only one affected.'

'Did the fingerprints show anything?'

'No. It seems whoever is responsible has been careful to use gloves. We can confirm that it was a one-sixteenth drill that was used to damage the brake line —and it was obviously a deliberate act.'

'But you've got nothing else?' Ginny asked.

'Well, when speaking to one of your neighbours ...' he paused as though searching for the name. 'Ah yes, here it is. Nigel Ward. He mentioned he had made an offer to purchase the property from you. Is there any reason you didn't tell us this fact?'

Ginny blanched, her eyes wide. 'I didn't think of it. Both he and my brother-in-law made offers "to take it off my hands" because they don't seem to think I'm coping.' She grunted and drew a breath. 'I didn't take either of them seriously and told them both I was not interested in selling—to them or anyone else for that matter.'

'Oh, I see. Fair enough then. How well do you get along with your brother-in-law, and your neighbour, Nigel Ward?'

'Nigel has been our neighbour all his life. He's an odd personality and not very social—so I guess we don't have much to do with each other.'

'What do you mean by odd?'

'Well, he's different. I know he has a flashpoint temper and has problems keeping staff, but, as I said, I have little to do with him.' Ginny held her breath, waiting.

'What about your brother-in-law? Are you close?'

'No. He and his family live about fifty kilometres away and we have always farmed our own places separately. I find him a little hard to get along with, and don't have much to do with him.'

'Hmm. I might go and have a talk to him as well.'

'Did you speak to Kirk?'

'Yes. I had a good chat with him but I don't think there's a problem there. He clearly has a good deal of respect for you.'

A flush of warmth washed over her and she smiled softly.

'So, is there anything else I need to do?' she asked.

'No. I'll keep you up to date on any new information and will be keeping the investigation open. Times are changing though, even in the more remote areas, so I would advise that you take all the usual precautions—you know–keep your vehicles locked and the keys inside, lock your house when you're not there, and of course, continue to check your property and stock on a regular basis. Perhaps you could keep a diary too? It often makes things clearer if there should be any further mishaps. And, even if a small incident does occur, please let me know.'

Ginny murmured. 'Sure.' She shared Donald's address with James and finished the call.

Huh! Mishaps? I reckon they were more than bloody mishaps.

AUGUST ROLLED on without further incident, and, days later, Ginny woke to a still, sunny sky, the temperature promising an early spring. Rolling up her sleeves, she dragged the pressure cleaner out of the shed and took it to the woolshed. Then, with the radio blaring, she switched it on and focused on blasting away a year's grime, dust, and mould from the inside of the building.

Almost finished, Ginny jumped, emitting a shriek when someone tapped her on the shoulder. She rounded in alarm and tripped over the cleaner. A strong pair of arms grabbed her and she looked up at Kirk's anxious face.

'Kirk. You frightened the life out of me!' She bent and switched the machine off.

He laughed. 'Sorry. I thought you would have heard my car.'

She shook her head and grinned. 'Nope.'

'I knocked on the house door but when you didn't answer, I had a walk around and saw your ute down here.'

'Not working today?'

'No. Neil and Valerie had visitors coming so we decided I'd have a day off. I could give you a hand if you like?'

She shot him a twisted smile. 'You're a bit late. I've

almost finished. The shearers will be here next week and I could do with a hand then, if you're not busy?'

He shrugged. 'Of course. I'll mention it to Neil tomorrow. How many days would you need me for?'

She grinned at the loaded question and bit her lip. 'Um, maybe three or four? The shearers will only take two days to do their job, but I need to have the sheep in the yards the day before—and then will need to treat them for parasites and worms before they go back into the paddock.'

'Sure.' He paused, his smile widening in the silence. 'With the weather warming up, I've discussed taking a week off with Neil. Want to head up to the Camel Hump if that's okay with you?'

'Oh. Sure.' She shook her head. 'I'm sorry Kirk. It's been so nice having you around, I'd forgotten you had your own agenda. I apologise. What is it you're searching for?'

He drew a deep breath and shrugged. 'I'm not really sure. I recently rediscovered a rock my grandfather had found up this way years ago. He told me he was coming back—but never got the chance. He died when I was a kid. Fell off the roof of a house he and my dad were building.'

Her hand rose to her throat. 'How awful for you all?'

They stood for a few seconds in silence, facing each other.

'So … is it okay with you?' he said. 'Going to have a look at the hump I mean.'

'Of course.' She angled her head. 'Want to join me for lunch and we can talk about it?'

'Thought you'd never ask. I've got a cooked chicken in the ute—and a container of potato salad. Not home-made though.'

'Oh—you've come prepared. I call that confidence.'

They both laughed and she shoved the pressure cleaner wand into his hand. 'You finish this and I'll wipe the windows off first.'

FILLED WITH A RENEWED LIGHTNESS, Ginny sat opposite Kirk at the Featherwood Station dining table half an hour later. They shared snippets of family, childhood, and the reason that had brought them together—the location of Kirk's grandfather's tin ore findings.

'There were heaps of mines around this whole plateau over a century ago but I doubt there's anything worth finding now.' She chuckled. 'I'm sure if there was, someone else would have beaten you to it years ago.'

'Yeah. I think my grandfather might have thought he'd struck the mother lode when he found that rock.' He shrugged. 'Anyway, I'd still like to have a look, even if it's to "walk in his shoes" as the saying goes. I think we might have had a lot in common ... had he lived long enough to find out.'

Compassion gripped Ginny and she placed her hand over his.

'Did you know the detective came to talk to me?' Kirk said.

Ginny sat back, nodding. 'Yes, he seemed to think you're an "alright fella".' She giggled. 'Not in those words of course.'

A shadow crossed Kirk's face. 'I reckon Stan thought it was me. After all, I'm the newcomer in town —and I know that usually brings with it a whole raft of questions and suspicions.'

Ginny tipped her head back and laughed. 'That's for sure. Don't worry—I've been warned about you.'

His eyebrows rose. 'So ... are you scared?'

She shook her head fiercely. 'Not a bit. After all, if you wanted to frighten me, you've had more opportunities than most in the last few months.'

He squeezed her hand. 'I'm pleased.' His voice was soft, almost a whisper and she could see his pulse pounding in his neck. Longing dithered at the edges of her conscience while the stress she hadn't realised she was carrying, rolled off her shoulders.

She resisted an urge to kiss him, instead, pushing her chair back and standing up. 'Coffee?'

'Please.'

Minutes later, Ginny drained her cup and heaved a

sigh. 'Well, much as I would like to whittle the afternoon away here, I need to check the windmill—and the cattle. The cows are heavy with calf now and will start calving soon. As soon as shearing's over, I'll bring them closer to the house.'

Kirk nodded. 'I've got nothing planned. Feel like company?'

Her heart skipped a beat and she grinned. 'Sounds great.'

THE OLD UTE RATTLED, restricting their conversation as they drove past the yards and up the rise toward the cattle while the dogs stood tall on the tray back, their ears pricked.

As they turned along the ridge, skirting bushland, Kirk pointed to the boulder on the crest of a hill a kilometre away. 'Is that what you call the cutting?'

'Yes.' Ginny gripped the steering wheel, her knuckles white. 'That's where Lyndon was when he had the accident.'

He faced her for a moment. 'If we have time, would you like to show me?'

She swallowed. 'Can do. We'll check the stock first, then go for a walk.'

A drive around the fence-lines confirmed all was well, the cattle contentedly grazing and the troughs full. They passed through the flock of now well-grown autumn lambs and their mothers before returning to the cattle yards almost two hours later.

Ginny slapped her wide-brimmed hat on and released the dogs. Then she locked the ute and dropped the keys into her pocket.

At Kirk's raised eyebrows she shrugged. 'Detective James told me to lock everything—so I am.'

'I'm pleased to hear it.' He reached for her hand and, together, they climbed the rough track.

At the top, they paused, breathing hard. Drum clung to Ginny's heels while the other four ranged back and forth, sniffing the ground and peeing at every opportunity.

Ginny pointed to the steep slope and the gently flowing stream below.

'It was here that the bike apparently left the track and rolled all the way to the bottom. I found Lyndon in the creek.'

'Did he drown?' Below his hat, Kirk's forehead was layered with deep creases.

Ginny shook her head. 'Apparently not. He had a head injury but they didn't find any water in his lungs so declared he had died of the injury and not by drowning.' She shrugged. 'I would have been pretty unhappy if they'd said he drowned seeing as we were in drought and the creek was barely a trickle at the time.'

'How awful for you.' Kirk rubbed a hand over his face. 'Was he not wearing a helmet?'

She grimaced and fought back the tears that threatened. He reached out and touched her arm.

'I'm so sorry. I didn't mean to upset you.'

'It's okay. That's the weird part of it all. He never rode the bike without his helmet—but on this occasion, we don't know what happened as he wasn't wearing it when I found him and despite searching everywhere, it has never been found.'

'Cripes. That is strange. What do the police say about that?'

Shrugging, she said, 'Not much. It's as much a mystery to them as it is to us.'

He bent his head, appearing to study his feet before shaking his head. 'Such a terrible thing to have happened in such a beautiful place.'

'I know.' She attempted a smile and faced him. 'On our way home, how about I show you the waterfall the dogs and I go to visit regularly. It's not far from the house but is not visible from the road or yards. When the kids were little, we used to take a picnic there at every opportunity in summer. They loved to swim and paddle about—and unless we'd had a lot of rain, it was quite safe for them.'

'Sounds lovely. Let's go.'

She smiled as he grasped her hand again and they trekked back to the vehicle.

It took only twenty minutes to walk to the waterfall and Kirk gasped. 'Wow! What a treasure to have on your place.'

'It is, isn't it. We're lucky—and even more fortunate that the creek was dammed on the other side of the village years ago, so the public go there and don't try to come onto our property.'

He winked at her. 'So it's only random southerners who ask to tramp over your place searching for abandoned tin mines then?'

She chuckled and squeezed his hand. 'Something like that.'

24

*A*fter Kirk left, an emptiness seemed to fill the house and Ginny was grateful for the phone calls that consumed her evening.

Claire announced that she had given notice on her unit and would be coming home in October, earlier if she could. Briony had secured a plane ticket for late November, stopping at Dubai enroute, and Mavis was delighted to report that both her Mah-jong group and the Art Gallery Management committee were now able to meet again in person.

'Would you like me to come and help with shearing, dear?' Mavis asked.

Ginny choked on a retort, imagining her frail, perfectly groomed mother sweeping stinky crutchings or chasing recalcitrant sheep around the yards. 'Thanks Mum. I've got help this year—and it's only for a couple of days anyway. Leave it until the girls get home and we can have a nice family get-together.'

'Oh, alright then. If I can help, you will let me know, won't you?'

'Of course.'

THE PHONE RANG AGAIN the following morning as Ginny was hanging the washing on the line and she ran inside to answer it.

'Hello?'

'Hello. Is that Ginny?' The woman's voice on the other end was unfamiliar and Ginny narrowed her eyes.

'Yes,' she said.

'It's Valerie O'Hara here—from Kallala. I'm sorry to bother you but Kirk was telling us you're shearing next week.' There was a pause.

'Yes. That's right.'

'I was wondering if you would think it terribly rude if my husband and I came to watch?'

'Oh, n-no. That would be okay.' Ginny answered.

'I've never been in a woolshed you see, and my husband is keen to set up a facility for visitors here—so I thought both of us really need to know what goes on. Perhaps we could help?'

Ginny dropped her shoulders. 'Yes, of course.'

Valerie chatted on and within ten minutes, Ginny smiled at the knowledge she now had an assistant with both catering and yard work. Ginny confirmed she would muster the sheep the day before. Providing morning tea, lunch, and afternoon tea for the three shearers, shed hand, and wool classer in addition to Kirk, Valerie, Neil, and herself would be their joint responsibility.

'What about breakfast and the evening meal? Do the shearers stay overnight?' Valerie asked.

'No,' Ginny said. 'They live close enough to drive out each morning and return to their families at night.'

'Wonderful. Well, I love to cook—so perhaps I could bring a bacon and egg pie and some scones and slices with me?' Valerie offered.

Ginny's eyes widened. In all the years she'd been on Featherwood Station, she'd only had help in the kitchen in those few years when the girls were both at home, and capable of being relied upon.

'That's very kind of you Valerie. I look forward to seeing you on Tuesday then—about eight o'clock?'

'Thanks Ginny. See you then.'

Ginny ended the call with a smile on her face. Her life had been too full for many close friends—and, except for Lola, those she had formed a bond with had moved away, seeking work and a better life in the bigger cities.

She picked up Sassy and stroked the cat's soft,

tabby fur. 'What do you think of that? We might have new friends if all goes well.'

THE WOOLSHED WAS BUZZING with activity when Ginny caught sight of the silver Mercedes driving slowly along the track toward her. She closed the gate behind the sheep and called to Kirk on the other side of the yards.

'It looks like Valerie and Neil are here? Will you greet them, or shall I?'

'Let's both go. We can spare a few minutes can't we?' he answered. Vaulting over the fence, Kirk's long legs reached her in seconds and, together, they approached the car.

The second Valerie stepped out of the vehicle, Ginny felt an affinity with her. Although slighter in build and perhaps a decade older, both women were of similar height and Ginny returned Valerie's beaming smile.

'Welcome to Featherwood Station.'

'Thank you so much for letting us join you today,' Valerie replied, her voice clear and warm. She turned to the man beside Kirk. 'This is my husband, Neil.'

Ginny smiled, wiped her palms down her jeans and shook his outstretched hand. 'Come into the shed and join the action.'

'I'll stay out here and pen the next lot up. Perhaps Neil can lend a hand out here after you've given them a tour?' Kirk said.

The pleasant-faced gentlemen in pressed jeans and clean shirt shot a grin at her.

'I told Kirk we're not here for decoration. Show us the way.'

Ginny smiled and led them into the shed. 'I'll introduce you to the team when we break for smoko.'

'Oh they're very disciplined, aren't they?' Valerie said as the three men lifted their heads and gave a brief smile or nod before continuing.

The shed hand raced along the board, picking up fleeces and throwing them onto the round, slatted table. While the wool classer, a pretty young woman, lifted her hand in a quick wave, spinning the table around and plucking the edges of the fleece, removing the stained locks.

Valerie stood perfectly still, clearly mesmerised by the speed at which both the young male shed hand and the woman operated while Neil rested a hand lightly on Ginny's arm.

'I'll go and help Kirk.'

Ginny smiled and let out a relieved breath. 'Righto. See you back here at half past nine for morning tea.'

He grinned and was gone.

She tapped Valerie on the shoulder. 'You stay here

and watch if you like. I'm going to push up more sheep.'

Valerie smiled in response, her attention now focused on the closest shearer, his deft sweeps with the handpiece removing the thick fleece, revealing a clean, white fuzz on the animal.

On the dot of nine-thirty, the buzz and clatter of the shearing plant stopped and a peaceful calm filled the shed.

'Valerie, would you mind helping me set out morning tea please?' Ginny removed the lid from a container of sandwiches while the workers took turns to clean up in the washroom.

In the corner of the shed, an urn bubbled on a small, cloth covered table, surrounded by mugs, a jar of coffee and a box of tea bags.

'Of course. I'll do the scones,' Valerie announced, deftly producing a plate full of fluffy white scones, half of them covered with butter and strawberry jam while the balance also had a large blob of whipped cream topping them off.'

Introductions were made, a plentiful supply of food consumed, and, thirty minutes later, everyone returned to their appointed duties.

The day flew and, as they trouped out of the shed late that afternoon, tired and dirty, Ginny glanced at the sky.

'Let's hope the rain they've forecast for later in the

week, holds off—or goes around us.' She grinned and crossed her fingers.

Valerie grasped Ginny's hand between her two. 'Thank you so much for today. It's been absolutely wonderful and I can't help thinking how lucky your children were to have been able to enjoy these experiences growing up.'

Ginny shrugged. 'Thanks. We've all loved it—and I'm sure will continue to.' She paused, a cheeky grin growing on her face. 'So ... are you coming back tomorrow?'

'Wild horses won't keep me away. Now I know the ropes, I'll go home and bake something tasty for tomorrow,' Valerie added.

Ginny turned to Neil. 'Yours and Valerie's help today has made things a good deal easier for me—and I appreciate it.'

'It's good to meet you, Ginny—and I have to say, I'm not surprised Kirk has prioritised your place over mine.' He chuckled and Ginny felt the heat rise up her neck.

She glanced at Kirk and he gave her a cheeky wink, his grin widening.

'It's called teamwork.'

And I'm delighted to have you as one of my team. Ginny stopped at saying the words aloud. Instead, she smiled while the flush of warmth cruised through her whole body.

KIRK LEFT on his hike two days later, a well-stocked backpack on his back with sleeping bag, a pick and billy strapped to the outside. When Ginny asked how he planned to cook his meals, he produced a bag containing a tiny gas burner and a collapsible pan, followed by a bag of rice and a few dehydrated meals.

'I'll build a fire where I can, but in case of rain, I've got this. Don't worry, I won't starve.' He indicated the long, thin bag propped on the floor of the passenger seat.

'Is that a gun?' she asked.

'Yes. I thought if I saw any rabbits up this way, I could supplement my diet.'

She pressed a palm to her chest. 'Glad to hear it. Feel free to dispose of any wild pigs you see too. They're the bane of a farmer's life—destroying everything they can, not to mention the native animals.'

Noting the gaiters strapped around his jean clad calves, she smiled approvingly. 'Good to see you're prepared for the scrub. I reckon the undergrowth will be hard going this year. No-one has been up that way for yonks and since the rain earlier this year, the track will be overgrown.'

'I'll be fine.' He gave her a quick hug, returned his backpack to his vehicle, and stood for a moment by the driver's open door. 'Back in a few days.'

'Okay. See you then.'

His smile was filled with a mix of worry and contentment. It was difficult having no mobile phone reception in the area, and, with no other means of communication, all she could hope was that he would find what he was looking for—and stay safe.

Rain fell in sheets as thunder rumbled the following afternoon. Catching up with office work, Ginny spent the day trying not to worry whether Kirk had found a sheltered spot to camp—and consulting the previous year's diaries.

She detailed the shearing figures, weight of the wool clip and estimated income and expenditure before moving on to the next event on the calendar— hay-making.

Rain beat against the window and she stared through it, comforted by the patch of blue emerging in the eastern sky, and the rainbow that hovered in the distance.

Perfect—just what the lucerne paddock needs. Humming to herself, she flicked through the address book until she reached W. Having rarely phoned Nigel —or his parents when they were alive, she hesitated. They had always been an intensely private family and the final words Nigel's mother had said, still baffled her.

Sucking in a breath, she dialled, surprised when her call was answered immediately.

'Hello?' Nigel's voice was cautious, measured.

'Hi Nigel. It's Ginny.'

'Yes.' Ginny flinched at his cool response.

'I believe you're now our local hay contractor?' She kept her voice light and friendly, uncertain of his comeback.

A few seconds of silence followed before he answered.

'I'm not sure about that ... but I've bought Terry Collins hay-making equipment if that's what you mean.'

She squirmed in her seat. 'Um. Yes. I'm sorry. I thought that meant you were taking over his business. Have I assumed too much?'

He grunted. 'Well—I wouldn't say that. I plan to expand my own hay sales and needed more equipment. But ... if you need your lucerne cut and baled, I'm happy to oblige.'

'Great. Thanks. Once this rain stops, I reckon the crop will grow quickly. As you know, it's my only lucerne paddock and if this summer treats us better than the last few, I'm hoping to get several cuts off it. If you could mow it as soon as it's dry enough, let me know when it's ready for baling, and I can help you. Would that work?'

'As I said months ago, I'm happy to help any time you need it.'

His voice had lost the hesitation of the first few seconds of their conversation and Ginny let out a quiet breath of relief.

'Great. I'll check the paddock regularly and let you know when it's ready.'

'Don't worry about that. I can have a look myself. Save you the trouble,' he said.

'Oh, okay.' She paused, suddenly apprehensive— she wasn't sure why.

25

*K*irk breathed heavily as he climbed a steep pinch and passed through the cutting. Turning back for a moment, he drank in the patchwork of orchards, market gardens and expanses of pasture. With his LandCruiser parked safely inside Ginny's cattle yards, he had no concerns of stock rubbing on it, and, with its taupe paintwork, it was barely visible.

Striding firmly, his mouth formed a close-knit smile at the condition of the track. He'd made good time, only occasionally finding himself amongst thick vegetation before the track opened out alongside a trickle of water that ran from granite crevices.

Evidence of wild pigs rooting in the softer areas and kangaroo and wallaby manure were everywhere—

and as he trod further from civilisation, stress rolled from his shoulders and he whistled softly as he walked.

After the limited assistance from Ned, he'd decided to keep his probing's to himself and, instead, drove to Stanthorpe and purchased a book depicting the area's history, in particular the tin mining era. He'd studied it in detail, his fingers cross referencing a number of spidery, dotted tracks indicated on the topographical map he had also managed to source.

Pausing to rest his aching knees after almost five hours of hiking, he glanced around the open, granite platform in front of him. Spindly trees and scrub grew from cracks in the surface and ground rocks formed a network of tracks. Shadowed by an overhanging rock-shelf, Kirk edged closer to what appeared to be a bottomless hole, wide enough for no more than one person—and a slim one at that. He shuddered as grim images of unsuspecting animals falling into the abyss crossed his mind—or worse, humans. Memories of Lola's comment about something bad having happened up here flashed through his head and his breath caught. *Did someone fall—never to be found again?*

Water trickled from a gap between boulders a few metres away and Kirk shrugged off his back-pack, fished inside it for an enamel mug, and held it under the flow. Unlike the brackish water further down where stock roamed, this was clear with not a speck of dirt to taint the contents of his mug. He sipped it carefully, nodding with approval and then gulped the balance as he gazed around.

Granite appeared to reach further west before dipping out of sight. After replacing his mug in the back-pack, he tucked his belongings against a clump of bush beside the track and set off to explore the immediate area.

Holes pocked the expanse of undulating ground and Kirk picked his way carefully amongst them. Some were wide—enough to allow him to scramble down a few metres–while most appeared to have once been mines of varying depths allowing no more than one or two people to enter at a time.

'I reckon this will make a good start,' he announced aloud.

In the midst of a clump of trees a few metres from the mines, an area appeared to have been cleared. Kirk viewed it appreciatively and kicked the animal manure from the site. Then he set up his flimsy tent, built a fireplace edged with rocks and filled his billy.

While he waited for the water to boil, he unfolded the map and followed the watercourses with a finger. Although not marked, he was certain his location had been part of an ancient batholith, worn over thousands of years to the current expanse of dirt and rock covered minerals. He reasoned its distance from the richer, more productive tin ore mines closer to civilisation would have reduced its popularity. Nevertheless, he accepted that, at some time, tough men had toiled to extract what they would have hoped, would change their lives.

Weariness caught up with him and he sluiced his head and hands under the water and cooked himself a meal. As the sun dipped in the sky, he parked himself on a flat piece of rock in the wide, smooth expanse of granite and watched a wallaby come to drink, a wedge-tailed eagle circle above—and eventually–the sun sink below the horizon.

Peace engulfed him. Returning to his campsite, he stoked the remnants of fire, wrapped his sleeping bag around himself, and replayed years of his life in his head.

'I reckon if you were still here Grandad, we'd be good mates,' he whispered. 'I wonder what you'd think of me coming here—leaving those I loved down south and beginning a new life altogether.' Ginny's smiling face drifted through his mind and he nodded. 'I think you would approve.'

THE DAYS PASSED QUICKLY, exploring the area and hiking to the farthest corner of what he assumed belonged to Featherwood Station, as he reached a taut boundary fence. Staring at the weed invested pockets of cultivation on the other side of the fence, it took a few minutes for him to realise that it wasn't a field prepared for barley or oats he was staring at. A tall tomato-like plant grew a few metres away, sheltered by a clump of bush and he grinned. This must have been where the marijuana haul was found. He shrugged and returned to the old mine site, fossicking amongst the rocks and rubble until darkness sent him back to camp.

Kirk woke to the sound of magpies warbling. He laid his food supplies on a rock after tidying his camp and expelled a grunt. A zip-lock bag held a couple of potatoes, carrots, and a wedge of cabbage from Ginny's vegetable garden.

'Hmm. All I need is meat.' After strapping his ammunition belt around his waist, he picked up the gun and crept quietly across the granite. A plateau of long grass shone in the early morning sunshine, so he tucked himself behind a clump of bush, and waited.

Within minutes, a rabbit appeared, followed closely by a second—and a third. While the rabbit-proof fence had been a success for generations, it was no longer manned or maintained and the dreaded, introduced pest had infiltrated Queensland.

'I'm doing the farmers a service,' he muttered as he pulled the trigger.

After checking the animal for signs of disease, he prepared it for the stew he would cook later in the day.

Then, having ensured the meat was well-wrapped and hung in a tree out of reach of wildlife, he donned his head-lamp and clambered into the largest of the ancient holes before beginning to chip with his pick.

Hours later, his shirt stripped off and thrown aside as sweat poured down his face, he dug up a rock the size of an eggcup, encrusted with opaque crystals. He turned it over in his fingers, excitement bubbling within him. Although small, he was sure this was what his grandfather had been talking about.

A rumble overhead startled him and he looked up, astonished at the heavy black clouds that had crept all around.

He quickly donned his shirt again, gathered his pick and jacket and returned to the camp-site.

Lightning slashed across the sky and thunder followed immediately. Kirk glanced at his belongings and hastily packed all he could into the waterproof pack. He struck the tent and rolled it tightly, lashing it over the top of his sleeping bag, then lifted the load onto his back, picked up the gun, and hurried to where, in the distance, he had found an overhanging ledge of rock.

'Let's hope it's big enough,' he huffed, breaking into a jog as the first spits of rain fell.

Seconds before he reached his destination, the

skies opened and the rain bucketed down, heavy, and cold, the needle sharp strands beating a tattoo on his hat. Dirt covered the bare rock floor and Kirk pushed himself hard against the entrance wall.

He fished out his head-torch and propped the back-pack on a rock inside the entrance. Squinting, his lips parted in amazement and he blinked rapidly.

The ledge above the entrance camouflaged the depth and breadth of the cave. Kirk switched on his head-lamp and explored deeper into the abyss.

A network of small tunnels led to dead ends. He tied a handkerchief over his nose as the stench of bat droppings filled his senses. Stepping around a wallaby carcase, he bent in half, wishing he had a crash helmet as his head bumped the rock above for the fourth time. With a sweeping glance, the beam of his light shone on an assortment of animal bones and he assumed at some point, the cave had been a lair for a family of dingos.

Despite his torch, the cave grew darker and he hesitated, turning back to the way he had come. Light filtered in from the entrance and he retreated to inspect the rain. It continued to pour, dropping in sheets outside and running down the granite in rivulets. Insulated from the noise by its thick roof of earth and rock, Kirk felt safe, as though where he stood belonged in a different world from that outside.

Bugger, I should have grabbed some dry firewood.

Minutes later, the storm eased. Kirk reached into his pack and drew out a second torch. Although small, it had a powerful beam, and armed with it and the headlamp, he returned to the depths, determined to discover where it led.

It didn't take long. He swung the torch light in a wide arc, pausing as the beam rested on a pile of rocks blocking what appeared to be another passage.

Crouching down, he pulled several aside, rolling them behind him as he continued. With his eyes adjusting to the darkened interior, he caught a glimpse of hessian sacks, bulging and tied at the top with baling twine.

He dragged one to the daylight and carefully opened it. Flashing his light on the contents, he paused as the beam reflected a sparkle. Leaning forward to inspect the rocks more closely, he sat back on his heels, a hiss escaping his lips.

'Oh my God. You were right Grandad! There is still plenty of tin ore here—but I'm not the first person to know that.'

His eyes narrowed. Someone had stored their find in the cave. Perhaps the rocks had sat there for years ... generations? But if that was the case, wouldn't they have been covered in layers of dust—and the hessian rotted?

Clamping the torch between his teeth, doubling

the strength of light, he returned to the rock pile and carefully moved the bags aside. Behind them, a random heap filled the passage entrance. Working quickly, he loaded his arms with as many rocks as he could carry and crept back to the daylight.

He stroked his beard as thoughts raced around in his head. These were different—larger and mostly whole. After inspecting them, he shrugged.

'Nothing startling here. Maybe a cave in years ago?' Shrugging, he gathered the rocks again, dug his gloves out of his pack, and returned them to the pile.

His curiosity grew. Scraping the wallaby skeleton aside, he dropped to his hands and knees and crawled into a smaller, narrow tunnel on the opposite side. A few metres in, once again a pile of various sized rocks greeted him. This time however, they were bigger and well settled into their surrounds. Even wearing the leather work-gloves, his fingers grew tender as he prised the lumps of granite, limestone, and various other unrecognisable rocks, away. For such a big man, the work was tedious, the space cramped.

Suddenly a large rock tucked to the side, gave way, and rolled to the floor, creating a cloud of dust. He crawled backwards as fast as he could. Thick dust filled his eyes, nose and throat and wracked with coughs, he retreated outside, and gulped the fresh air.

Waiting for the dust to settle in the tunnel felt like

waiting for Christmas as a child and he massaged his temples and stretched. Eventually, convincing himself he was doing the right thing, he pulled on his gloves, switched both the torch and headlamp on, and returned to the tunnel.

In the beam of light, dust motes floated around him. He lay on his stomach, the pile of rocks to one side, and shone the torch slowly around the small cavern. A flash of white set into the wall caught his eye and he crept closer. *Quartz?* He pulled off his glove and ran his hand along the fissure, noting its disappearance into the earth at the back of the opening. Something sparkled and he held the light still, squinting as he studied the stone.

Breath whistled through his teeth as he exhaled. He gazed at the veins of yellow and gold. Most were thin, like spider veins. But as he crept closer, his torch shone on a thicker, solid band of yellow that vanished into the undug portion of tunnel.

Gold? Perhaps it wasn't the tin ore his grandfather had found—but something even more valuable.

As evening fell, Kirk spent the next hour ensuring the rocks were replaced in a way to appear untouched before returning to the entrance. He stretched and picked his way to a shallow water hole, stripped off and, shivering, washed the dust away. Then, too tired to bother with a fire, even if he'd had dry wood, he prised open a tin of tuna and ate it. Then he spread out his bedroll and lay back, his hands behind his head, listening to the scuffling of small creatures in the dark.

A wallaby paused at on a rock a few metres away and stared at him. He grinned back and spoke softly. 'Wait until I tell Ginny about this.'

26

*G*inny was pleasantly surprised to see Nigel's ute parked next to the lucerne paddock only two days after their phone discussion.

Mounted on Akela, her intention had been to check on the soon-to-lamb Dorset ewes. Hesitating for a few seconds, she swung the mare away from the track and rode down the slope to what Lyndon had named 'The Hundred Acre Paddock', after his favourite childhood storybook "Winnie the Pooh". Being relatively flat and clear of vegetation, the paddock made a perfect hayfield and for the past few years, had served them well, despite recurring droughts.

Waving as she drew near, she called out.

'Nigel!'

He raised his head and stood perfectly still as she approached.

'What do you think? Dry enough to cut?' she asked.

He removed his hat and wiped his forehead. Ginny's eyes widened at the sight of the long, lanky hair. She had not seen him without a hat since Lyndon's funeral, and on that occasion, his small stature had been scrubbed and suited, his straight, black mop trimmed and neatly combed, accentuating his olive complexion and dark, almond-shaped eyes.

'Yes. I'll get to it this afternoon. I have a paddock of my own to mow so I'll do yours straight after.'

She nodded. 'Okay. I could help. I can use our tractor and the old hay rake Lyndon used.'

'No. Leave it to me. My equipment is quicker and more efficient than yours and when it's baled I'll get my workers to stack it in your shed.'

He nodded curtly and walked back to his vehicle.

Grunting, she shrugged at his change of mood— from willing cooperation a few days earlier, to authoritarian.

'Thanks for your help, neighbour.' She whispered and chuckled. *Lyndon was right. You are an odd bod.*

NIGEL ARRIVED on Featherwood Station later that afternoon, driving a new John Deer tractor and towing a red hay mower-conditioner straight through the creek.

Ginny had been tidying the woolshed following the carrier's removal of wool bales that morning—providing what she hoped would be a sizeable chunk of the year's profits in due course. As she swept the locks of wool strewn around the shed into a pile, she looked across the valley and pursed her lips as the mower-conditioner swayed drunkenly behind the powerful tractor.

Dripping water from the wheels, the green monster halted and Nigel climbed down the ladder on the side of the vehicle.

Ginny leaned against the windowsill in the shed, her eyes narrowing.

Years earlier, when Lyndon's grandfather had been at the helm, and relations had obviously been better between the farmers, a concrete ford had been constructed at the bottom of the creek adjoining Featherwood Station and Glenrowan. Although now eroded in a few places, rocks had filled the pockets, providing a perfectly usable method of crossing from one property to the other without having to follow the road, saving time and distance. Although unused for decades, Ginny admired Nigel for his ingenuity. For the large wheels of a tractor, the ford was a good alternative—although towing expensive hay-making equipment through water, even if it was shallow, would not have been her choice.

While Nigel seemed to take forever to conduct

what Ginny could only assume was a check of the equipment before he began work, a smirk touched her mouth briefly and she turned to the dogs, lying silently on the loading dock.

'I wonder how long it will take for Donald to find out my hay is being cut?'

The tractor roared into life again and she waited, wishing she had the binoculars with her as the vehicle progressed slowly around the outside of the field. Letting out a huff, she returned to her sweeping, before, satisfied the shed was as tidy as it needed to be, she leant the broom against the back wall, closed the windows and doors, and strode to the house.

In the early spring air, the hum of the heavy diesel engine and rhythmic thump of the mower drifted toward the homestead. The sun was setting before it stopped hours later. Waiting until tail-lights had traversed through the gates on both sides of the crossing before disappearing along the track toward Glenrowan, Ginny strode to the paddock to inspect the crop with Drum at her heels. The sharp, sweet scent of freshly mown lucerne greeted her and she bent down and gathered a handful. After inspecting the leaf content and thickness of the stalks, she held it to her nose, breathing in slowly and smiled.

'Perfect.'

Terry had welcomed any help both Lyndon and she had given him over the years, and through him,

Ginny had gained a good knowledge of the important stages of turning the rich, green legume from a swathe of fresh alfalfa to nutritious blocks of dried hay.

She wondered how much Nigel knew about making lucerne hay—and a sliver of unease crept inside her. Dropping her handful of cuttings, she looked down at Drum.

'I guess I have to trust he knows what he's doing because he cuts his own.'

OVER THE NEXT TWO DAYS, Nigel dragged the equipment back and forth across the ford, raking the hay. As it was tossed into the air, falling softly in a loose heap behind the rake, Ginny kept an anxious eye on the weather forecast. Rain had been predicted again but, so far, they had been lucky and the clouds had dissipated before they reached the ground.

Relief filled her whole being when, late the following evening, she watched the green tractor begin its slow journey around the outside edges of the crop, and the kathump-kathump sound of the baler wafted across the land.

Darkness fell and Ginny took her plate of steak and vegetables out onto the veranda where she could see the lights circumnavigate the lucerne paddock. A second set of headlights arrived in due course and she scraped a hand through her hair with nervous repetition. Voices carried in the night and she relaxed slightly, knowing the neatly packaged bales were being picked up. She crossed her fingers—hoping Nigel had tested the moisture content in the finished bales before having them stacked in her shed. Baling this soon was fraught with the danger.

Her concern over the moisture content in the already shedded hay, grew as the morning progressed. She strode up and down the veranda, remembering the fire on a farm a few kilometres away. It had been enough to understand the importance of not stacking hay too soon as the heat generated was easily ignited, destroying not only the crop, but the building in which it was stored.

AT TEN O'CLOCK THAT EVENING, the drumming of rain on the roof coincided with silence in the paddock.

Ginny paced up and down the veranda, peering through the rain as the lights moved quickly away, fading behind the row of trees on the Glenrowan side of the creek.

It rained all night and Ginny knew it would be days before whatever hay still lay on the ground would be dry enough to bale. Even then it would have lost much of its leaf and the quality poor.

She sagged against her pillows as her chest tightened. While she accepted it wasn't a disaster—there would be many opportunities for repeat crops before next winter arrived– hope had buoyed her along. Determined to prove to everyone, including herself, she was an efficient and successful farmer was paramount to ensuring Featherwood Station remained in her family—the family that consisted of Briony, Claire and her–and not Donald or Andrew.

FINE WEATHER FOLLOWED AND, with no sign of Nigel arriving to rake the remaining lucerne, Ginny's frustration—and concern–piqued.

She hoped Kirk was safe and enjoying his solitude in the bush. 'I bet Kirk knows all about hay-making.' She smiled at the cats as they glanced at her with apparent disinterest.

Striding to the cupboard, she removed the moisture metre, taking care not to damage the long wand as she removed it from the case. The battery was flat so she put it on the charger and decided to mow the lawns while she waited for it to charge. After whizzing around the yard on the ride-on mower, she tidied the equipment away and returned to the veranda. Then, picking up the binoculars that rested on the outdoor table, she peered through them, and released a hiss of frustration at the still silent paddock. Snatching the moisture metre from the bench, she strode to the old hayshed at one end of the lucerne paddock. Constructed from ancient hardwood, Ginny loved its "A" framed roof and wide doors that opened outwards. Inside smelled of freshly baled hay and she inhaled its sweet scent. She waited until her eyes adjusted to the poor light before plunging the wand into the closest bale. Noting each reading, she progressed through a dozen or more bales and huffed in disbelief.

'You haven't got a clue, have you Nigel.'

The moisture content was so high that she spent the next hour pulling bales off the pile and separating them around the shed in the hope they would dry without the risk of spontaneous combustion. Then, as her dismay increased, she hurried back to the house to quench her thirst. Chewing her lip she stared at the dogs lying in a pool of sunshine on the lawn and made her decision.

'Back to your kennels I think. I'm going to have a word with my so-called hay contractor—and give Akela some exercise while I'm at it.'

She closed the gates behind Flute, Banjo, Harp and Chime and looked around for Drum.

'What's the matter, mate?' The little dog angled his head, his gaze pleading and she grinned. 'Oh, alright then, you can come too.'

Then she caught and saddled Akela, strapped her

helmet on, and rode away with Drum at the mare's heels.

AKELA WAS fresh and she danced for the first kilometre before settling into a brisk trot. Ginny followed the roadside outside Featherwood Station before turning onto an old, gazetted road that linked several of the more used and gravelled accesses to other farms in the area. There were other ways of approaching Glenrowan, including via the ford beside the lucerne paddock, but it was a nice day and Ginny was enjoying the sun on her back.

Nigel's packing shed was quiet, the row of cabins behind it where the pickers stayed, appearing abandoned. *Where are the haymakers?*

Her concern grew as she approached Nigel's house. It had been over two years since she had visited. On that occasion, the lawns had been mowed and the Photinia hedge trimmed and tidy. Now it was so high and thick it was impossible to see the house.

She dismounted and tied Akela to the post supporting a rickety gate that had once welcomed visitors—and entered the yard. The grass was longer than a crop of wheat and her eyes widened.

'Nigel!' Ginny called and waited, listening for any sign of life before knocking at the front door.

With the exception of a solitary bird call, there was no response. She walked around the house with Drum at her heels, calling as she went.

In the far corner of the yard, a wooden tool shed leaned against the fence, its window covered with cobwebs and dust and the rough door standing ajar. She returned to the front door and knocked again. An eerie quiet resonated from the filthy veranda and she shrugged and returned to her horse.

A whimper sounded, followed by yipping and she glanced around for Drum.

'Come on boy!' She gave a whistle and waited, hooking Akela's reins back on the post and returning to the house yard. The whining continued and she frowned.

'Where are you?' she called, following the sound until she rounded the corner and paused, listening. From inside the shed, Drum's cries reached her and she ran toward him. Throwing the door wide open, she halted, startled by the dog's ferocious scratching and pitiful yips.

'What is it?' She bounded forward, pushing past a dust-covered lawn mower, and knelt in front of the old metal trunk. Drum's cries were disconcerting, his quivering unfamiliar and she lay a hand on his shoulder. 'It's okay, mate. Shush now.'

The little dog looked up at her, his ears pricked— and then his gaze returned to the trunk.

Ginny looked around and, satisfied no one was watching, cautiously lifted the lid.

A towel lay over the contents and she slid it aside, gaping in silence. Drum began whimpering again, leaning on her as he, too, stared.

She fell back onto the dirt floor, her legs too weak to hold her. With her hand over her mouth, she pulled the sleeve of her shirt over her fingers and lifted the red motorbike helmet to inspect it more closely. The name "Lyndon" was written across the back in gold paint, and on either side was a row of glittery stickers Ginny had watched her girls attach years before. Holding her breath, her mind voiced denial.

Her gaze moved to the hessian bag in the trunk next to where the helmet had been. Carefully prising it open, she ogled the rocks and wondered why they would be there? A ray of sun struggled through the window and Ginny picked up one of the stones and held it close to the light. It shone, its crystalline streaks pale against the dark of the rock. She put it back in the bag and sat, crossed-legged on the dirt floor with her arm around Drum.

As her head cleared, she replaced the helmet, and lay the towel over it, carefully ensuring everything was as she found it.

Then, grabbing Drum by the collar, she stumbled to the gate, unhooked Akela's reins, and dragged herself onto the mare's back.

'Home Drum. We've gotta get out of here. Run!'

She kicked Akela into a brisk trot and headed along the back road toward Featherstone Station, her heart thumping and whispering the words to the beat of the horse's stride.

'No! It can't be?'

27

*A*kela broke into a gallop as though sensing Ginny's urgency. Blood pounded in Ginny's head and she glanced behind her as she rode.

Ginny's hands grew clammy on the reins and she grabbed a handful of Akela's mane as the ground rushed past. Desperate, she calculated how far it was until she reached the safety of home, attempting to swallow her fear. Estimating another two kilometres, she suddenly remembered the cross-country fences. When Briony was competing in Eventing before she left for Scotland, Lyndon had removed the top wire and replaced a wide section with a smooth horizontal pole, providing both horse and ride with a safe—and solid, jump.

It had been years since Ginny had attempted riding over even the smallest of poles on horseback—but now, that fact barely crossed her mind. Steeling herself, she glanced up at the red-brown kelpie streaking over the paddock ahead of her and gathered her reins.

'Come on girl. We've got this.' Akela flicked an ear as though understanding what was required of her and steadied to a rhythmic canter as the fence loomed. She propped briefly and tucked her front legs under her as they rose. Ginny stood in her stirrups and leaned forward, clutching the horse's mane as they sailed through the air.

Landing smoothly on the far side, Akela gathered momentum, her hooves thudding on the earth as they raced for home.

The homestead came into sight at the same time as Frank's white mail van. Ginny had never been more thankful to see both in her life.

Her arms shook as, dizzy with relief, she watched Frank turn into her driveway and approach the house, one arm waving frantically out the window to her.

Slithering to a halt beside his vehicle, it took Ginny a few seconds before she could speak. Akela's sweaty flanks heaved, froth flicking from her mouth and she dropped her head.

'What the hell's going on?' Frank said. 'I saw you galloping down that hill behind the house as though a swam of wasps were after you.'

'Frank!' She panted. 'It's Nigel.'

'Nigel. What about him?'

Before she had regained her breath, Frank had switched the engine off and helped her dismount.

'Now, take a few breaths and tell me what this is all about.'

At that moment, the rumble of a diesel engine sounded from the direction of the cattle yards and Ginny's heart leaped, her body shaking uncontrollably.

Kirk's vehicle appeared from behind the rise and Frank grabbed Ginny's arm as she wobbled with giddy relief.

The vehicle stopped beside Frank's and Kirk got out, his forehead creased.

'What's happening here?' His eyes roved over the two of them before staring at Akela. 'Geez. Looks like you've been chased by the devil,' he snorted. Then his face grew serious. 'Something is wrong, isn't it?'

Ginny nodded, drew a deep breath, and told them about the hay that hadn't been baled, her determination to find out why, and Drum's subsequent discovery of Lyndon's helmet.

'Good God!' Frank rubbed his face with both hands, his gaze flicking from Ginny to Kirk. 'We need to let James know.'

'You take Ginny inside, Frank. I'll unsaddle this mare and give her a rub down.' Kirk glanced around as he reached for Akela's reins. 'Where's Drum?'

'I don't know. He was like a rocket. Once I told him to go home, he ran like the wind and was ahead of me.'

'Hmm. I'll check the kennels as we walk past. You never know, he could be back in his pen by now.' Kirk shot Ginny a soft smile and led the mare away.

Before she and Frank reached the veranda, a whistle halted them in their tracks.

'He's okay. Lucky you left his kennel gate open— he's hiding in his bed,' Kirk yelled.

Ginny sighed. 'Thank goodness he's alright. Poor little fellow must be so traumatised.'

'We'll get a cup of tea into you first, then ring James. Then you can worry about the dog,' Frank said matter-of-factly, his snowy head bobbing.

Ginny sank into a chair, grateful for Frank's no-nonsense approach. Disbelief still consumed her and for a moment, she thought she might wake from a terrible nightmare. But then Frank passed her a steaming mug of tea and she knew it had been far from a dream.

JAMES ANSWERED IMMEDIATELY AND, with the phone on speaker and laid on the table in front of them all, Ginny downloaded the days events as precisely and methodically as her brain would allow.

'I see. Are you alone, Ginny?' James' tone was kind but efficient.

'No. Both Frank and Kirk are here with me.'

'Good. I'll apply for a search warrant immediately and we'll get a team out there as soon as possible. Stay inside and I'll be in touch.'

'Okay, thanks.'

Ginny clicked the "end" button and drew a deep breath.

Frank nodded, his lips clenched in a thin line. 'At least he didn't dilly-dally. Good to have an efficient copper to deal with.' He picked up the phone and glanced at Ginny. 'Okay if I ring Lola? She'll be wondering where the hell I am.'

'Of course. Go right ahead.'

'I'll make another cup of tea.' Kirk pushed his chair back and Ginny gave him a grateful smile.

'Sorry, Kirk. I haven't even asked how you got on in the bush. Did you enjoy your break?'

He chuckled. 'I reckon you had a good excuse to forget about everything except your adventures these past few hours.'

It wasn't until they were sipping their drinks that Ginny asked again. 'So ... did you find what you were looking for?'

He raised one eyebrow. 'Maybe. I found a cave. When it rained, I moved camp to keep dry. Turned out it was a good decision.' Pausing, he grinned at Ginny.

'And?'

'I found some hessian bags filled with rocks. I think they could contain tin ore—and I think that's what my grandfather mentioned when I was a kid. Strange though, these look to have been bagged quite recently —well, certainly not thirty-five years ago anyway. The track up there wasn't as overgrown as I expected either.

Ginny froze, her mug half way to her mouth. She lowered it to the table again. 'You said hessian bags?'

'Yes. You know ... sacks like those used to pack potatoes.'

'That's weird. In the chest where I found Lyndon's helmet, was a sack of rocks too. It wasn't full.' She huffed a breath. 'Wouldn't have fitted in if it had been.'

Frank cleared his throat and both Ginny and Kirk stared at him. He rubbed a hand over his chin, frowning. 'Do you think Nigel could have been up there and found something he considers valuable?' He grunted. 'I can't imagine him wasting time on anything that he didn't think would be profitable.'

Kirk inclined his head. 'Possibly. If it's minerals he wanted though, all he had to do was obtain a mining licence—and get permission from the land-owner for access.'

Silence reigned for a moment as realisation dawned and they stared at each other.

'He offered to buy Featherwood Station from me. Do you think a few rocks containing a bit of tin ore could have been his motive?' Ginny shrugged. 'Sounds a bit far-fetched to me. I understood the majority of minerals were stripped from this area over a century ago—and there's nothing much left now?'

'Hmm.' Frank sniffed. 'Could be he doesn't know that though. No one around here knows him very well, but from what I've heard, Nigel's never done anything unless there's something in it for him.'

'When Flora Ward was dying, she asked me to keep an eye on him. I never understood what she meant.' Ginny said.

A dog barked and all three of them jumped, leaping to their feet.

'It's Lola.' Ginny smiled and opened the door to greet her.

'Stay here, love. I'll go. She said she'd bring dinner for us all.' Frank pushed passed Ginny.

Shadows lay in the garden and Ginny turned to Kirk. 'It's later than I thought. James said I wasn't to leave the house, but the dogs need feeding and the chooks locked up for the night.'

Kirk rested his hands on her shoulders and met her hazel eyes. 'I'll do it. You stay here with Lola and Frank in case James rings.'

She nodded. 'Thanks.'

He leaned forward and kissed her gently on the lips before disappearing out the door.

Heat rose up her neck and she pulled her collar

tight as Frank and Lola entered. With arms reaching, Lola hugged Ginny while Frank unpacked a cardboard carton onto the kitchen bench.

'You poor love. What a day!' Lola said.

Ginny grimaced and stepped back to meet her eyes. 'It certainly has been action-packed. I'm anxious to hear what they find at Glenrowan though. Maybe once we know what's been going on, the reason for recent events will be clearer.'

'Right. Well, while we wait to hear what the police find, I suggest we get a hot meal inside us all. It could be a long night.'

While Lola bustled about in the kitchen, Ginny set the table and found a bottle of wine. 'I think we deserve one tonight. Agree?'

Both Frank and Lola smiled at her as Kirk's footsteps clumped onto the veranda.

'I agree,' they said in unison.

28

*A*t ten o'clock that night, lights shone through the kitchen window as a vehicle approached the homestead.

'This will be James—I hope.' Ginny pushed herself out of the squashy couch and strode to the veranda as a car door slammed.

James smiled at her and Ginny's hopes rose. 'Come inside. Would you like a drink? Or some dinner? We have plenty.'

'Thanks Ginny. A cup of coffee would be nice, but I won't hang around. Thought I'd brief you on what we've found.'

'Of course.' She indicated an empty chair and James plonked himself into it.

'You know Frank and Kirk—and this is Lola.' Ginny

could barely contain herself and perched on the edge of her chair. 'Did you find it—the helmet I mean?'

James nodded. 'We did. Thanks for ringing so promptly.' He sat forward, his hands clasped together and resting between his knees. 'We've conducted a thorough search and the team will be back tomorrow in daylight to ensure they haven't missed anything. In addition to the helmet, we also found a drill with a one-sixteenth bit fitted. It appeared to have brake fluid on it—and was beside a roll of black insulation tape. Indications are they are the same as those used on your truck. Oh, and we also took a pair of boots which we believe match the imprint taken at your yards.'

Ginny covered her mouth with her hand and Lola groaned.

'So you think Nigel did it?'

James nodded. 'We've taken him in for questioning.' He sculled the mug of coffee and reached forward to put the empty cup on the table.

'Before you go, I think you should know what I found during my few days exploring the old miners site at the back of Featherwood Station,' Kirk said.

James sat upright. 'Go on.'

Kirk relayed his discovery of the rock-filled bags. 'From the description Ginny gave of the hessian bag and rocks in the trunk with the helmet, I think those I found were the same—or similar.'

'Oh. So you think there may be a connection?' James asked.

Kirk shrugged. 'I don't know—but it makes sense. Those at Nigel's may have been taken as samples. Hessian deteriorates quite quickly and, if the bags in the cave had been filled and stored years ago, wouldn't they have fallen apart by now?'

'Good point.'

'Not only that—I dragged one of them into the light, and noticed it was relatively new.' Kirk paused, narrowing his eyes. 'The other odd thing was the track I followed to get to the mine site appeared to have been used more recently than I'd expected.' Kirk added.

'Hmm. 'I'll bear that information in mind. Thank you.' He rose to his feet 'I'll be off then—and will keep you informed.'

Kirk followed Ginny and James to his car. As the taillights disappeared down the driveway, Kirk wrapped his arms around her.

'Are you okay?'

Taking a deep breath, she relaxed and smiled up at him. 'Do you know, I am. I'm exhausted but I reckon I'll sleep better tonight than I have for months.'

'Good.' He stepped back and looked down at himself. 'I think I'd better get down to the cottage and have a good scrub.' He grinned and sniffed an armpit. 'Yep, that's essential.'

They both laughed and walked back to the house, hand in hand.

Frank greeted them at the door. 'I'm heading home now.' He inclined his head toward the kitchen where Lola was putting away the clean mugs. 'Lola insists on staying the night to ensure you're okay.'

Ginny glanced sideways at Kirk, catching his cheeky wink.

'I'll be fine, Lola. Honestly.'

'You've had a horrible few months and I'm not going to leave one of my best friends on her own if I don't have to.' She folded her arms across her chest. 'So I'm staying.'

'Right. Well—glad that's cleared that up. See you tomorrow.' Kirk grinned at them and leaned toward Ginny. 'I'm going into town tomorrow to pick up the kitchen bench I ordered for the quarters. Then I'll be here for a couple of days getting it fitted for you.'

She clapped her hands together, her face alight. 'Fabulous. A good night's sleep followed by much awaited progress on the quarters. What more could a girl want.'

Kirk followed Frank down the steps and both Ginny and Lola trailed behind.

'I'll be back in time to open up in the morning, so don't you worry. Feed that little possum for me will you?' Lola planted a smacking kiss on her husband's cheek and stood beside Ginny.

As the vehicles drove away, a Boobook owl hooted. Standing arm in arm, the women remained in the soft, evening air of spring for a few minutes before turning toward the house.

Lola patted Ginny's hand. 'Into bed for us both I think.'

'Sleep in Claire's room if you like. I gave it a good clean and made up the bed a couple of days ago. Who knows, she could turn up any time.' Ginny held her hands up and chuckled.

'Goodnight, sleep tight.' Lola yawned and wandered down the hallway.

Ginny checked Flute was tucked into her bed on the veranda and locked the doors. Then she walked softly to the bathroom, showered, and fell into bed. She thought she would have fallen asleep immediately but she didn't. Instead, she lay on her back, staring at the patterned, pressed-metal ceiling above her.

Although relieved the worst was over, a myriad of questions still played through her mind. Nigel's motive was yet to be revealed—and the question still hung in the air. Did he find the helmet somewhere—or was he involved with Lyndon's death?

GINNY WOKE EARLY the next morning. She trod quietly to the French doors, wrapped in a dressing gown, her feet bare. Dawn hovered in the east, its pink rays mixing with the soft gold of sunshine. She heard the kettle whistle and smiled. *Lola's already up.*

Dressing quickly, she tidied her bed and brushed her hair. Then, with a wide smile on her face, she greeted her friend.

'Here you are, dear. Coffee and a piece of toast to get you started.' Lola handed her a plate and mug and returned to the stove. 'I'm cooking us both scrambled eggs and bacon. It's time you got a decent breakfast into you.' She looked Ginny up and down and smiled.

'Thanks Lola. You're a Godsend.'

'Right. Well, once we've eaten, I'll give you a hand with the chores.'

'I'll be fine Lola. You don't need to stay.'

The older woman shook her head firmly. 'I may not need to, but I want to—at least until we hear from that detective and know what motive was behind that slimy little creep's actions.'

Ginny grinned meekly and took her coffee and toast onto the veranda.

At eight o'clock the phone rang and Ginny snatched up the receiver.

'Hello?'

'Ginny, it's James.'

Ginny touched the speaker button before answering. 'Hi. How did last night go?'

'Surprisingly well actually. My colleague and I

conducted the usual interview and Mr Ward was more cooperative than I expected. Evidently he hasn't been sleeping and was quite remorseful.'

'Really! That's good isn't it?'

'Of course. It doesn't change his case though. I'd like to advise he has been charged with manslaughter, wilful damage, and acts endangering life. The manslaughter charge relates to your husband and the other charges to the damage of your truck and the life-threatening position he put both you and your cattle in with the windmill incident. He wouldn't own up to the kerosene spillage under the woolshed, but we're certain it was him.'

'Manslaughter. Gosh. That's awful. So what happened?'

'He admitted arguing with your husband. Said he met him when he was returning from a mine site on your property—which means we can also charge him with both trespassing and stealing if you wish to pursue that line. He offered to buy the block of land containing the old mines and Lyndon refused. Admitted he lost his temper and, when Lyndon turned away from him, he picked up a rock and threw it.'

Ginny frowned. 'But the helmet? Why wasn't Lyndon wearing it?'

'According to Mr Ward, Lyndon removed it and got off the bike while they were talking. After he'd thrown the rock, Lyndon fell sideways and rolled down the hill. Mr Ward said he checked him for signs of life but realised he was dead, so he left him and climbed back to where the bike was parked and pushed it down the slope to ensure it looked like an accident.' He harumphed. 'It appears Mr Ward has quite a temper— we've collated a few minor complaints about him from previous staff.'

'I wonder why he wanted to mine though. If there's good money to be made in tin mining, why haven't some of the big companies been sniffing around?' Ginny shook her head. 'I don't understand.'

James shrugged. 'I admit I don't either. However, he did mention he had to look at alternative income streams. It appears he's struggled to get vegetable and fruit pickers since the start of the pandemic—and didn't have family to help like some of the other farms.'

'That's true. I thought that was why he was going into hay-making. Although it used to require helpers to get the hay stacked, these days machinery can do most of it.' Ginny slumped in her chair, her head spinning. 'Oh my goodness. That's hard to take in. He's been our neighbour for ever—and went to school with Lyndon and his brother.'

'I know how you must feel, Ginny, but at least now you can rest easy. Of course there's the court case to go —and probably a million questions you will want to ask, but all in good time.'

Ginny let her breath exhale with a whoosh. 'Thanks for letting me know, James.'

'Not a problem. You take care now and I'll keep in touch.'

'Thanks. I appreciate it.'

She replaced the receiver and turned to Lola. 'You heard that?'

Lola's eyes were wide as she shook her head. "Didn't I tell Kirk these little country towns often have secrets.' She twisted her mouth and looked at Ginny. 'Mind you, I never expected it to be quite so serious.'

Plonking herself on a chair, Ginny mulled over the conversation with James.

'Nor me. God. Who would have guessed that all this was going on in Featherwood Falls—and right next door!'

29

*A*fter Lola's departure, Ginny trundled around the dogs, chooks, and horses, completing her daily chores in a daze. While disbelief still hovered, the reality of the past eighteen months sank in slowly and she relived the two incidents that made her want to retreat into a foetal position and crawl into bed—the day she'd found Lyndon and the discovery of his helmet.

With the warmth of spring soaking into her bones, tension gradually eased and the black spots that had been hovering in her vision, disappeared.

Around mid-morning, Kirk arrived and Ginny rushed out to meet him.

He stepped out of the vehicle and her smile widened. They hugged and she breathed in the clean, fresh scent of soap and shampoo as she clung to him.

After a minute, she pulled back and met his warm, dark eyes. Newly cut hair and a trimmed beard had transformed the wild-looking bushman of last night, to a handsome gentleman—despite the navy blue and denim work clothes.

'Are you okay?' His voice was thick with emotion.

'Yeah. I think so. Getting my head around it all anyway. What about you?'

'I'm fine ... and I'm keen to hook into getting these quarters finished and spick and span so you can start having visitors come. I think people are champing at the bit to get away from home after all the restrictions —and what better place for a claustrophobic city family to come to than Featherwood Station.' His smile faltered as a shadow passed over her face. 'I know it's all a bit daunting for you but trust me.'

'You're right. It's one of those jobs that has been worrying me. And now I can rest knowing what happened to Lyndon—even if it does still make my blood boil–I want to finish the project that he was so enthusiastic about.'

He hugged her briefly before returning to his vehicle, a new spring in his step. 'Come on then. Let's get this stuff unloaded so I can make a start. I need you with me so we get it exactly the way you envisaged.'

Her heart leapt with gratitude and she clambered into the passenger seat as they shared a laugh.

THE FOLLOWING days were filled with more hope and happiness than Ginny had felt for a long time. As the new kitchenette took shape, she sanded and stained a long, narrow timber table that Lyndon had made for this very project. With a combination of old wooden chairs they had picked up at a clearing sale, the veranda turned into a comfortable outdoor lounge— perfect for visitors to sit and enjoy a drink and nibbles. While the evening sun bathed the western horizon, the patchwork of crops, plantations and native bush unfolded in front of them.

'I reckon that's it—done,' Kirk announced.

Beaming with delight, Ginny took a deep breath and gazed around the neat little kitchen. Protected from the weather by clear glass on two sides, the sunny, yellow-painted cupboards shone while the new cooktop and sink sparkled. To the side of the building, Kirk built a fire-pit. While Ginny drove the tractor, they manoeuvred two of the largest logs they could find into position around it and stepped back to admire their work.

Ginny dusted off her hands. 'I don't know about you, but I reckon it looks pretty darn cute.'

Kirk chuckled. 'Yeah. I love historic buildings—and this is a perfect mix of old and new. I reckon between you and Valerie, you'll be pulling the tourists to this area in droves.'

She giggled. It seemed as though the final load that weighted her shoulders, had lifted—and she could now look forward, instead of backward.

'I've got something to tell you.' Kirk's voice deepened as he caught her hand and dragged her to sit on the log beside him.

'Ah-oh, that's sounds ominous.'

'Sorry. It's not meant to be. Quite the opposite I hope.'

Her skin tingled as a heaviness filled her insides. *He's leaving.*

'I'm going to have to go back to Dalgety.'

The weight inside her grew and her eyes prickled. 'I thought that might be coming.'

'Hey. Don't be sad. Hear me out.' He reached for her jaw and turned it to face him. 'I had a call from Mrs Coonan's family. They've decided to sell the property and have offered me first option to buy.'

Her eyes widened. 'Oh! What did you say?'

'Yes. It's a nice little house and has good bones. Needs some TLC but I can do that ... and I've discovered I want to live here.'

Ginny's tentative smile widened as he continued.

'I'm going to have to sell my house in Dalgety to buy it, so, as soon as the paperwork is completed here, I'll head south and get myself sorted out. Neil and

Valerie want me to continue as their maintenance man, and it seems there's plenty of work around this district for an honest, hard-working builder.' He grinned, anxiety pulling at the edges of his mouth. 'What do you think?'

'What do I think.' Ginny paused, pressing a finger against her cheek, feigning contemplation. Then she returned his grin. 'I think it's a great idea.'

'Good.' His shoulders lowered and he stood up and reached both hands toward her.

She allowed him to pull her to her feet and they gazed at each other in silence.

'Christmas,' she said.

'What about Christmas?'

'You'll be back here by then, won't you?'

'I sure hope so. I've already been onto the health department to find out what permit I need for border crossing—and I think I need to act quickly and get back here before they change the rules again. Why?'

'I think after all we've been through, we should make this one to remember. The girls will be home. Maybe we can invite Neil and Valerie and Lola and Frank, Mum—and even Ned?'

Kirk's head tipped back and a deep jovial laugh filled the air.

'Good luck with that one. But yes, it would be wonderful to meet your family and for them to be here with you after all you've been through.'

'Good.' She pointed to the two cane armchairs on the veranda of the quarters. 'Stay here. I'll be back.' Then she turned and ran toward the house.

Minutes later, she reappeared with a tray containing a bottle of champagne, glasses, cheese, and crackers.

He stepped forward to take it from her and rested it on the table. 'Celebration?'

'I reckon so. The mystery of all those frightening incidents have been solved, we have absolution for Lyndon's unnecessary death—and now we have the beginnings of a whole new business.' She waved an arm. 'Not only that. The seasons this year have given me so much optimism for farming, and I know I can do it.'

The cork popped and Kirk poured the wine, then handed her a glassful.

She angled her head slightly and touched her glass against his. 'It's early days, but I have a suspicion we've both got lots to look forward to.'

'I'm sure of it. To Featherwood Falls—and us.'

30

*G*inny looked around the crowded room. Fairy lights twinkled along the veranda eaves and the lamps in the garden cast shadows amongst the roses.

Filled with laughter and excited chatter, the homestead glowed warmly, as though encompassing all those within it with love and safety. In the corner, a tree towered toward the ceiling, tastefully decorated with silver and gold baubles, glittering pin-pricks of light and around its base, a pile of colourful gifts covered the floor.

Her gaze rested for a moment on her daughters—vivacious brown-haired Briony who had grown into a beautiful and confident woman. Claire, the quiet one who looked so like her father. Tall, thin and fair-haired, her love for animals and fierce determination would see her through any hurdle—of that Ginny was certain.

Two Christmases ago, it had been just the five of them—herself and Lyndon, the girls, and her mother, and none of them could have imagined what was to come. *How life can change in the blink of an eye.*

A small smile played around her mouth as snippets of conversation reached her. While Briony chatted animatedly with her grandmother about the pitfalls of social media, Claire appeared patiently absorbed in Ned's opinion of the governments management of Covid19 and morose tales of ghosts. What ghosts had to do with the pandemic, Ginny wasn't sure. Kirk had been sitting with Neil, Valerie, Lola, and Frank. Now he stood up and moved over to stand beside her.

'Everything okay?'

'Everything is perfect. Thank you for being here.'

He clasped her hand and squeezed it gently. 'Thank you for letting me into your life.'

Before she could respond, Briony whispered in her ear. 'Grandma and I are starving. Let's get dinner on the table.'

She chuckled and shrugged apologetically to Kirk.

'I'll carve the turkey,' he said.

With a wide assortment of vegetables, ham and condiments covering the table, everyone shuffled into place, touching elbows, and commenting about the feast laid in front of the. Claire filled everyone's glasses but, before they began eating, Briony rose to her feet and tapped her wineglass with a fork.

'Attention please everyone.'

Eyes swivelled to focus on the attractive, brown haired woman, so similar to her mother—at least in looks.

'I'd just like to say a few words. As you all know, this year has been a hard one for the whole world. None of us have been able to live the way we used to, and I for one, realise I have always taken so much for granted. Being stuck on the other side of the world made me aware of how much I missed this place and missed being here to support Mum through what I'm sure have been the toughest two years of her life. Claire and I both feel the same. We're so grateful to be home, safe on Featherwood Station and incredibly grateful to you all for your friendship, support and love.'

Claire stood up then and grinned at her sister. 'Enough of the waffle Bri.' Her gaze swept around the table. 'We'd like you to raise your glasses for a toast.'

The clink of glass, coupled with a smattering of approving comments filled the next few moments before Claire spoke again.

'To friends, both old and new.'

'To friends.'

The murmur escalated into cheery chatter as Briony added, 'And a special welcome to Kirk. I've no doubt your arrival in Featherwood Falls would have caused a few raised eyebrows, especially when it coincided with the weird goings on here.' She paused. 'But since we've had the opportunity to get to know you over the past few weeks, both Claire and I would like to let you know—we both approve.'

Briony's cheeky grin encompassed them all and Ginny turned to Kirk. He clasped her hand under the table and she returned her gaze to her daughters. A tentative smile spread into a wide beam as she read the love and acceptance in their eyes.

She squeezed Kirk's hand in return and the last doubts that had hovered, fell away, leaving her filled with the knowledge that everything would be alright.

ACKNOWLEDGMENTS

No book is complete without thanking the many assistants who help in its creation. While writing, researching and finding inspiration, I am grateful for every suggestion, correction and piece of information that goes into my stories to make them strong and enjoyable.

I would especially like to thank my husband for his patience, beautiful meals and constant assistance—especially with the mystery and crime scenes. I could not have done it without your vast knowledge and experience of Policing.

To Lauren at (CREATINGInk), thank you so much for your ongoing, professional editing skills, and to Patti Roberts (Paradox Book Covers) for your beautiful book covers.

To my sisters and children, who are my constant support—thank you from the bottom of my heart.

To you, dear readers, I hope you enjoy your visit to Featherwood Falls. Thank you all for reading.

ALSO BY HEATHER REYBURN

Tullagulla Series

The Cedar Tree

The English Oak

The Pepperina Grove

A Tullagulla Christmas

Fantail Ridge Series

Peninsula Promises

The Lupin Fields

The Scent of Promise

Featherwood Falls Series

A Stranger in Featherwood Falls

Secrets in Featherwood Falls

Sparks Fly in Featherwood Falls

Clouds over Featherwood Falls

SECRETS IN FEATHERWOOD FALLS

A small country town. A conscientious cop. And a whole lot of secrets.

Constable Rhys Morton is new to Featherwood Falls and knows one thing for certain—he wants to remain in this village as much as he wants to remain a cop. But just as he uncovers troubling historical information, an accusation threatens his security and he must weigh up his options. Should he pursue the cold case and risk ruffling powerful feathers, or protect his future and a budding romance?

Claire Shepherd is still reeling from her father's death and when fresh heartbreak strikes, she seeks peace in the haven of Featherwood Station, her childhood home. Sparks fly between Claire and the new cop in town and she is torn between her dream of managing her father's legacy or falling for a man whose position is only temporary.

Alarm bells chime when new neighbours move in. Is this little town the sleepy hollow Rhys believed it to be? Desperate to uncover local secrets, he seeks Claire's help. After all, she knows the area and he has nothing to lose—except his heart.

Secrets is Rhys and Claire's story and the second in the Featherwood Falls series.

SPARKS FLY IN FEATHERWOOD FALLS

Fed up with life under scrutiny, Ashleigh Paton considers her grandmother's favourite saying— *"Escape to the Country! A Change is as good as a holiday."*

The advice ignites a yearning in Ashleigh to leave city life and all it involves. A teaching position in Featherwood Falls could provide the answer, one she hopes will offer the new life she craves. After all—what could go wrong? It's better than being unemployed and the reward could be the peace she desires.

Damian Cartwright has a secret. Like his eccentric great-aunt, a reclusive life in the bush suits him. Except now his son, Charlie, is old enough to start school, and old enough to be subjected to ridicule. It's time for action, even if that involves calling a truce with Charlie's feisty new teacher.

When unexplained events occur in the area, young

Charlie forces Ashleigh into seeking answers. But uncovering the truth proves more shocking than imagined and sparks fly in more ways than one.

Can Ashleigh extinguish the inferno without destroying all she has gained? Or will her dreams be over before they begin?

Sparks Fly in Featherwood Falls is book three in this series.

CLOUDS OVER FEATHERWOOD
FALLS

In a town teaming with secrets, three women find themselves inexplicably entwined.

At the edge of her future, sixteen-year-old **Zoe** teeters, uncertain. The vibrant city with its dazzling lights, familiar sounds and scents, exudes adventure and a dream career. But when unexpected tragedy strikes, she is left to navigate the world on her own, gripped by loneliness and fear.

Lola is feeling the weight of her years. Despite a loving husband, a flourishing business and a circle of faithful friends, something is missing. While she pours her soul into a menagerie of sick and abandoned animals, her heart aches for the return of her only child.

At forty-two and lonely, **Emma** is free at last. Lost love and an unwavering commitment to her late mother have confined her to the quiet charm of Featherwood Falls. And while her role as teacher's aide at the local school fills her days, she longs for something to happen—something that will transform her existence and redefine her life.

Can Featherwood Falls offer the key to uniting these women? Or will a dangerous voice from the past destroy family bonds, challenging the discovery of love and hope.

Clouds over Featherwood Falls is the fourth book in this series.

ABOUT THE AUTHOR

Heather Reyburn enjoyed an idyllic childhood in beautiful New Zealand, before settling on the Darling Downs in Queensland. With a passion for nature, animals, reading and all things farm related, it wasn't long before her rural lifestyle inspired dreams of writing stories of her own. She loves happy endings, history, suspense, and characters who remain with the reader long after "The End". When not writing, Heather is often found in the garden or spending time with her husband and family.